MONTANA DAWN

**Center Point
Large Print**

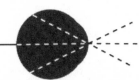

MONTANA DAWN

Stone Wallace

CENTER POINT LARGE PRINT
THORNDIKE, MAINE

This Center Point Large Print edition is
published in the year 2011 by arrangement with
Avalon Books, an imprint of Thomas Bouregy & Co.,
Inc.

The text of this Large Print edition is unabridged.
In other aspects, this book may vary
from the original edition.
Printed in the United States of America.
Set in 16-point Times New Roman type.

ISBN: 978-1-61173-027-2

Library of Congress Cataloging-in-Publication Data

Wallace, Stone, 1957–
Montana dawn / Stone Wallace.
  p. cm.
  ISBN 978-1-61173-027-2 (library binding : alk. paper)
  1. Nevada—Fiction. 2. Female offenders—Fiction.
    3. Large type books. I. Title.
PR9199.4.W3424M66 2011
813′.6—dc22

                                                    2010050681

This book is dedicated with affection
and gratitude to Chelsea Gilmore

The Editor every author hopes to find

Center Point Publishing
600 Brooks Road ● PO Box 1
Thorndike ME 04986-0001 USA

(207) 568-3717

US & Canada:
1 800 929-9108
www.centerpointlargeprint.com

PROLOGUE

The Day Before . . .

Hunter Tipton was the publisher and principal writer of the *Colfax City Chronicle*. It was a small circulation newspaper servicing a weekly readership of around eight hundred, even though the city of Colfax, Nevada, boasted a population of just over two thousand people. The simple truth was that there was not much news to report. Little of interest ever happened in Colfax.

Until recent events piqued public interest.

Unlike many in his profession, Tipton was not a drinking man, but today as he sat down to write his column he replaced his usual strong black coffee with a bottle of whiskey, which he poured liberally into his caffeine-stained mug. He consumed his drink in a single swallow.

He needed the fortification that alcohol would provide. His thoughts were troubled. Tomorrow morning the hangman would arrive in town to officiate at a publicly applauded execution that was slated for noon.

Throughout his early career as a reporter on big-city newspapers, Hunter Tipton had witnessed the cynicism that had developed in many of his colleagues. Tipton had vowed that he would

7

never permit himself to compromise his own journalistic principles. He maintained an honesty in his writing, never realizing how difficult a task that could often be. Today he would put his integrity to a test.

Tipton stared at the few words he'd jotted down with eyes that were tired and rheumy. He studied his brief composition before he grabbed the sheet of paper and crumpled it, tossing it carelessly at the side of his desk. He heaved a breath and leaned back in his chair, the wood creaking as he pushed it back from the desk. His eyes veered outside the big *Colfax City Chronicle*–lettered window that overlooked the main street. A street now virtually empty except for a few people meandering around the gallows—built for one purpose but which would now serve another. The citizens of Colfax had raised an uproar over being cheated out of a hanging and demanded the right to see that the gallows would still be put to good use.

And so tomorrow come noon the whole town, and probably the better part of the county, would be out. Tipton could barely contain his disgust. He recognized the hypocrisy of these church-going, God fearing people. Perhaps they had a right to be present at the hanging, but to him it was a ghoulish proposition. What bothered Tipton most was how these good folk would behave tomorrow come noon. He anticipated them casting aside their facade of self righteousness to reveal their true colors: taunting the condemned and then cheering as the trapdoor was swung open. He knew that there would be no dignity afforded the prisoner in those final moments.

Tipton considered his own hypocrisy. He was quick to pass judgment, but was he really any different from his friends and neighbors and those who would be traveling great distances to watch the barbaric taking of a life? Though certainly motivated by curiosity or the vicarious need for revenge, they could at least justify their presence by saying they were witnesses to justice being served. But Tipton's motives were distinctly different. He would be profiting from the execution. The story would be printed in tomorrow's newspaper as a special late edition. By delaying the publication until after the hanging he was guaranteed of a good day's readership. Probably the best in the paper's short history. His business was barely surviving and he needed a good story to sell newspapers, which his coverage of the execution promised to provide.

But . . . he couldn't leave it at that. To perhaps take the sting out of his own conscience Tipton decided he had to write beyond what was his "duty." He knew more. He would tell more.

He slid his chair forward to his desk and

poured himself another generous splash of whiskey. He reminded himself that as a journalist, yes, he had a responsibility to his readers. But he also felt another responsibility. An obligation, really. He owed the condemned a final service: to write the story fairly, without bias or embellishment. Without the sensationalism he knew his readers would want.

He made up his mind that he would leave it to others to tell the "legend," their dime novel presentation colored by their own conclusions. He would write the truth. The truth behind the story of the "Outlaw Queen" known as Montana Dawn.

He touched the tip of his pen into the inkwell and started to write:

It was said that she was given her name because she entered the world at sunrise, a brilliant sunrise, under the wide, clear skies of a Montana autumn.

Tipton leaned back and took a long, critical look at his opening paragraph until he felt satisfied that it could not be improved upon. Then he sighed, redipped the pen in the inkwell, and prepared to go on.

Before he could continue, the door to the office swung open and Tipton looked up from his work to see the marshal, Jake Braddock, enter. Tipton suppressed his annoyance at the interruption and instead expressed a muted surprise at the unannounced visit by the marshal. Braddock had only been city marshal for a very short time and while they had met briefly at the jailhouse and had seen each other around town, this was the first time the marshal had come by personally to see him.

Very quickly Tipton understood. Braddock appeared uncomfortable, and did not hide his discomfort well. His naturally ruddy complexion was somewhat paler and the creases in his face and forehead were deeper and more pronounced. He wasn't a squeamish man; after all, in his capacity as Marshal through various appointments in the Southwest he'd presided over his share of hangings. But he'd earlier confessed that he had never been present at the hanging of a woman, and it clearly troubled him. Tipton assumed that he just wanted someone to talk to, though he didn't view it exactly as a social call. Reluctantly, Tipton obliged him.

"Busy, Mr. Tipton?" the Marshal asked.

Tipton pushed back in his chair. "Nothing that can't wait, Marshal," he said amiably.

Braddock was a fat, middle aged man whose love of food and especially great quantities of beer was made evident by a large belly that flopped over his trousers like a carelessly discarded sack of flour. Tipton noticed that Braddock was holding a mug of beer that he'd brought over from the saloon next door.

"Hot day," Braddock said by way of explanation. For effect he brushed away imaginery perspiration from his brow with his free hand.

Tipton nodded. There was an uneasy silence between the two men before Tipton brought himself to ask: "How's she holding up?"

Braddock inhaled a raspy breath and replied: "Seen men who don't take it as well."

The marshal walked over and thumped his great weight down on the side of the desk.

"Maybe I should be asking how *you're* holding up?" Tipton remarked.

Braddock swallowed some beer and wiped the foam from his full, drooping mustache.

"Got a job to do," he said simply.

"Not an enviable one," Tipton said.

"No, it ain't," Braddock agreed with a heavy sigh. "First official duty in Colfax and it has to be somethin' like this. But 'least I won't be springin' the trap. Coulda done it for hundreds of scoundrels without battin' an eye. But—not this one. Bad enough just bein' there to see it's done right."

"To satisfy the will of the people," Tipton said with a bitter edge.

Braddock's jaw muscles flexed. "She was judged fairly by the court, Tipton, you know that."

"Didn't mean any offense," Tipton said with a defensive brush of his hand.

Braddock nodded absently. "Gotta put aside the fact that she's a woman," he said. "She committed crimes even some men put to death ain't done. In the eyes of the law, guilty is guilty."

"Suppose we all have to convince ourselves of that," Tipton said, shifting in his chair.

"You sayin' she ain't responsible for what she done?" Braddock said brusquely.

"No, I'm not suggesting that at all," Tipton returned. "But, Marshal, you know as well as I that public opinion in this matter has been one-sided. She was judged guilty even before she went to trial."

Braddock's eyes took on a hard look.

Tipton picked up his pen and tapped its end against the surface of the desk. He said: "And because of that, for tomorrow's paper, I decided I'm not going to just write about the hanging. I want to tell the whole story—all the facts, as I know them."

Braddock frowned. "As *you* know them?"

"Yes, from the various reports I've read . . . and from what Dawn herself told me when she asked for that interview."

"Heard you weren't going to print that," Braddock said.

"Let's say I've had a change of thinking."

"What purpose will that serve?" Braddock asked suspiciously.

"To present her as a person," Tipton stated firmly. "She's entitled to that."

Braddock's penetrating gaze remained fixed.

Tipton went on. "The way I see it, people have got to look at her as some kind of . . . inhuman beast. That's the only way they can justify hanging a female. You know, Marshal, it's funny. A man steps up to the gallows and it's all right for folks to feel a little sympathy for him. The product of a bad childhood, maybe an abusive upbringing. Usually some quirk in his background that made him turn mean. Something that people can grasp. But for a woman to be hanged . . . why, human nature being what it is, people can't allow themselves room for compassion. To accept that kind of extreme punishment folks have to regard her as someone without any redeeming qualities. They don't want to look any deeper for a cause. Just a bad seed, they say. Then they can feel satisfied that they exterminated her rightly, like they would a mad dog. That's what I mean about public opinion being one-sided."

Braddock snorted. "So—you wanta be tellin' the other side of the story. Maybe write 'bout the *good* she done."

The marshal was clearly not an educated man. He seemed to have a basic way of looking at things, likely cultivated from his years as a lawman, and Tipton understood that most of what he was trying to get across to him went beyond Braddock's comprehension. He was someone who would take Tipton's words and filter them to their simplest component.

"That's not what I mean," Tipton replied carefully. "It's not my intention to turn her into some kind of a martyr. But, like all of us, Marshal, no person is simply all black or all white."

Braddock drew a deep, wheezing breath. "Talk like that ain't gonna make what I got to do any easier."

He finished his beer and hefted himself from the side of the desk, hitching up his trousers. Tipton noted that the marshal didn't look any less uncomfortable than when he first came in. But Tipton also knew it wasn't his place to pacify Jake Braddock's conscience.

Still, he spoke his final words with a confidence intended for Braddock. "I'm sure you'll get through it fine tomorrow."

Braddock cast his eyes toward the open whiskey bottle on Tipton's desk and arched an eyebrow.

"Maybe we all will," he said.

After the marshal left the office, most probably to refill his beer mug, Tipton slowly shook his head and gazed back at his writing. The marshal's visit had interrupted his train of thought and he again studied his opening paragraph to get his brain back on track. But it was difficult. His talk with Braddock was another reminder that the public was less interested in the facts than the fiction that surrounded Montana Dawn's brief life as an outlaw. Maybe he should indulge himself to that second cup of whiskey he'd poured. Alcohol could free the pen as effectively as it freed the tongue. But he decided against it. At least for now. The liquor might mellow him to the point where a blatant bias might creep through in his words. That would surely offend his readers, already stained with a prejudice.

No, he could not do that to them. More importantly, he could not do that to *himself.*

Finally, after long, thoughtful consideration Hunter Tipton once more set about writing . . . though with the sad and bitter knowledge that whatever words he composed—if they were remembered at all—would only serve as a footnote to the legend of Montana Dawn.

CHAPTER ONE

It was said that she was given her name because she entered the world at sunrise, a brilliant sunrise, under the wide, clear skies of a Montana autumn.

Her folks were prosperous cattle ranchers and the girl, an only child, whom they had christened Montana Dawn Prescott, enjoyed a privileged life. Pretty and fair skinned skin with petulant, full lips and soft, doe-like chestnut colored eyes, she was remembered by those who knew her as a happy girl, if quiet and introspective, and one possessed of intelligence and an active imagination. She was a voracious reader and particularly enjoyed stories that took her to faraway places and sent her on glorious adventures.

But her childhood abruptly ended when she was twelve. That was when her father innocently ran afoul of a neighbor who responded to a presumed insult by shooting him dead. Montana Dawn's mother was devastated; the girl became withdrawn. She had loved her father dearly, but as she stood at the snow swept graveside, motionless, her long strawberry blonde hair soft in the bright sunshine, blowing in the cold breeze, watching as the simple pine coffin was lowered on ropes into the ground, she neither felt nor expressed any emotion. The mourners' sympathy turned to a strange curiosity as the young girl's blank stare was noted by each in attendance.

Unable to maintain the upkeep of the ranch, her mother lost the property to a ruthless land-grabber named Sefton, who just happened to have an acquaintanceship with the man who had killed her husband, who himself had been spared penalty for the crime due to Sefton's political influence.

Montana Dawn's mother died just several months later, of an unspecific cause that many whispered was simply a broken heart. She was just thirty-four. The girl was sent to live with relatives, who received her reluctantly since they had many children of their own, and who quickly found they were unable to deal with the sullen child who never smiled and who rarely spoke.

Then, after just two years, the girl left the house one morning to go off to school and did not come back. Her relatives were relieved rather than alarmed, and, if truth be told, put little effort into locating her.

Her childhood and the memories it carried were forever behind her.

At the age of fourteen, Montana Dawn had become a woman.

For the next three years Dawn—as she preferred to call herself—traveled, eventually heading south since she could no longer tolerate the long, cold winters she had enjoyed as a child in Montana. She worked at odd jobs, mostly waitressing in lunch rooms and restaurants where the tips were good, moving on once she had accumulated enough money to continue her journey. In the spring of 1883 she found herself in Colfax City, Nevada. It was her plan to move on west to California.

At the time of Dawn's arrival, Colfax had taken an economic downturn with the decline of the mines, which had provided the city with most of its financial importance as a freight and staging center. While Colfax had developed sufficiently enough not to be wholly dependent on the once-booming mining trade, the population had begun to drop off as citizens and miners alike traveled to other destinations to work their trade. The advantage was that where once there was little respect for law and order, the departure of the restless miners and other rootless and ofttimes ruthless individuals who had come to Colfax seeking quick riches resulted in the community adopting a peaceful, quiet lifestyle. Decent folk could at last feel safe and protected.

Dawn traveled to Colfax by stagecoach. Her traveling companions were an elderly woman and her granddaughter, who was just about

Dawn's age, and who shared Dawn's quiet appraisal of the other during the long ride from Utah. The girl was proper and pampered, dressed in a Quaker bonnet that framed golden curls and fine clothing, and Dawn thought only momentarily that if life's circumstances had turned out differently she might have been looking at an image of herself. The other passengers were a recent widower who explained that he was going to Nevada to live with his son and daughter-in-law; and a talkative wares salesman who focused much of his conversation on the two young girls, though having a difficult time choosing which one to favor.

Dawn departed the stage without good-byes and collected her luggage. She had enough money for a few nights' lodging but sought a boardinghouse where meals would be provided at a minimal charge, rather than staying at a hotel and dining at restaurants.

She found accommodations at Mrs. Potter's rooming house, which included a free breakfast and twenty-five-cent dinner, and the next day she got a job performing double duties as a waitress and dishwasher at the Central Hotel restaurant.

By this time Dawn had worked in enough restaurants to know she did not want to pursue such mediocre and low-paying work as her life's ambition. But at the age of seventeen with only a few years of schooling, she remained aware that she lacked sufficient skills to place her aspirations any higher, particularly in the towns she traveled through, where opportunities for women were scarce. She harbored the hope that California might offer better prospects. That part of the country was booming and she'd heard that the opportunities were plentiful. While the stories Dawn read as a child and her own daydreams had fueled her with the wanderlust to someday cross the ocean to foreign locales, visiting places with such exotic names as Tahiti and Singapore, circumstances dictated that she become more pragmatic in her plans, and the future she had hoped for herself now exceeded no farther west than Sacramento or San Francisco.

She figured she would need to work only a month to put together a stake that would see her on the final leg of her journey.

But then fate intervened . . .

She met him that first week she had come to town, on a sunny Saturday afternoon when she was out taking a stroll and wandered into Harley's Mercantile.

Jed Harley was the proprietor of the establishment. He was a tall young man with fine features and wavy sandy-blond hair that he kept impeccably groomed. He was busy with a customer but immediately took notice of the girl perusing the merchandise in the store. He was familiar with many of Colfax's residents but had never seen the girl before and so was intrigued by the attractive stranger. One thing he took note of was that while most of the city's women-folk wore bonnets or fancy hats when outdoors, this girl had no head wear and her long straw-berry blonde hair flowed free and easy down over her shoulders and splayed across the back of the pale blue dress she was wearing. He hastened to fill his customer's order before the girl could leave, and once he put the cash from the sale into the till he walked over to her.

"Is there anything I can help you with, miss?" the young man asked.

Dawn turned her eyes toward him and responded with a timid smile. "Just looking."

The girl stranger seemed shy, or perhaps preoccupied with her thoughts, and so Jed decided to let her be.

"Well, if there's any way I can be of service, just ask," Jed offered politely before returning to the counter.

Dawn smiled again and continued browsing through the merchandise. She perused the dry goods and assorted knickknacks stocked neatly on the shelves with no particular interest. Jed assumed she was just passing time.

After a while it looked like the girl was getting ready to leave. Jed had been quietly watching her, periodically lifting his eyes from the paperwork he had been pretending to busy himself with. His furtive glances told him that although she was young, probably just a teenager, there was a maturity about her, reflected most prominently in her eyes, which had a sad look about them. Jed dealt with enough people through his business to form pretty accurate observations. In the girl's case he determined that she had probably gone through some rough experiences in her life.

Dawn stopped at the door. "You have a nice store," she said.

Jed had hoped for the opportunity to initiate conversation and replied hastily, "It was my father's. I took over after he died. Reckon I'll never get rich, but it's a steady living."

Dawn nodded and gave a smile, and again she turned to the door.

Once again Jed quickly spoke up. "If you don't mind my asking, miss, are you new to Colfax?" He explained the reason for his perhaps personal question. "It's just that I've never seen you in the store before, and I know most of the people in town."

Dawn paused before answering. "I'm newly arrived," was all she said.

"You aiming to settle here?" Jed inquired gently.

Again Dawn hesitated and Jed looked instantly apologetic. "I'm sorry. Maybe I'm asking too many questions."

Dawn's demure smile grew wider, setting Jed at ease. "I don't mind," she said. "Actually this is just a stopover. I'm planning to move on to California."

"California," Jed mused. "Traveling alone?"

Dawn nodded.

"Family out there?" Jed asked next, assuming that was the only reason a young girl would be journeying by herself.

Dawn just gave her head a slow shake. Jed didn't pursue the matter, detecting that the girl wasn't of a mind to discuss her plans. She said good-bye and left the store.

But during the next couple of weeks Dawn would occasionally stop by the mercantile and Jed gradually became better acquainted with her—if slightly. She remained a quiet girl, spoke few words, and she learned more about Jed than he did of her. But Jed enjoyed her visits, however brief they most often were.

They did share introductions and Jed was intrigued by her name: Montana Dawn Prescott. Dawn explained how she had got her name but said that she simply preferred to be called Dawn. Her legal birth name, Montana, had always struck her as sounding tomboyish, and one of which she was not too fond. Jed, however, continued to address her as Miss Prescott, and she too remained formal, referring to Jed as Mr. Harley. It seemed proper in their acquaintanceship.

Then one day Dawn came into the store and, following her usual casual browsing, mentioned to Jed that she would be leaving Colfax at the end of the week. The time had come for her to continue her journey west to California.

Jed had forgotten about those plans she had told him when she had first come into the store some weeks before, and he was taken aback by her announcement. He tried not to show his disappointment, though he could tell by the somewhat curious way she looked at him that he was not concealing his feelings very well.

Dawn responded humorously to his downcast expression. "Mr. Harley, if I didn't know any better, why, I'd say you're almost sorry to see me go."

Jed waited a moment before summoning the courage to confess. "Reckon I am, Miss Prescott."

Dawn smiled—an enigmatic smile.

"What I mean is, it's been nice having you come around the store," Jed added swiftly.

"I don't know why you would say that," Dawn said in a sincere tone. "I haven't been much of a customer."

Jed gave his head a tilt. He didn't know how to admit what he really felt: that he had become quite attracted to the girl.

"It's not your patronage I'll be missing," he finally said, quietly.

"Oh?"

"No, it isn't that at all," Jed continued, fidgeting. He made himself go on, though fumbling with his words. "I, uh—well . . ." Finally he breathed out in exasperation.

Dawn hid her amusement at his awkwardness.

Jed tried again, forcing himself to get the words out correctly. "Well, Miss Prescott, I'd like to close up shop for about a half hour and maybe step out for a cup of tea. I'd be greatly honored if you'd agree to accompany me."

Dawn surprised him with her answer. "I think I'd enjoy a cup of tea, Mr. Harley."

She could see the relief that quite visibly passed over him, like a pressure-filled balloon releasing air, and the smile that she had been suppressing finally came to the surface.

Now Jed was smiling too. Grinning, in fact.

He suggested the Mayfair Restaurant. Before they left the store Jed walked over to one of the shelves and secreted an item inside his coat pocket, his furtive gesture catching Dawn's eye and arousing her curiosity. Then he doffed his townsman's hat and followed her out the store, affixing the CLOSED sign to the inside of the window and locking the door behind him. They strolled the two blocks to the restaurant, making idle conversation while passing couples on the street who walked arm in arm. Jed rather envied them, though he gentlemanly resisted the urge to be so presumptuous with Dawn. Therefore he was surprised, pleasantly, when Dawn herself looped her arm around his. He didn't comment but could not suppress the proud smile that crossed his face as he met friends and customers along the way, enjoying the appraising and mostly approving looks of people who knew Jed Harley only as a quiet bachelor not known to keep company with the ladies. Their arms remained interlocked until they finally entered the restaurant and took a seat at one of the tables, next to the big window that filtered in the warm afternoon sunshine. The restaurant was quaint and quiet with a setting more intimate than the dining room at the Central Hotel.

Jed felt relaxed. He offered to buy the girl lunch but she said that just tea would be fine. Jed decided it good manners to also decline a meal, though he was hungry and would have appreciated a piece of sweet apple pie, which was a house specialty.

For the most part it was a quiet time. The girl still seemed shy, possibly a little guarded, and Jed respected her reticence. Until he remembered the little item he had taken from the store. As they were finishing their tea Jed slipped his hand inside his coat and withdrew a small bottle of perfume.

Before handing it to her he said: "I've noticed you looking at the fragrances when you come into the store. I'm just sorry I didn't have the time to wrap it proper."

Dawn looked surprised—and puzzled. She seemed reluctant to take it. "I don't know if I can be accepting a gift, Mr. Harley," she said primly. "After all, I hardly know you."

Jed raised a shoulder. "Well, consider it a going-away present. Or a good luck token, if you'd like."

Dawn's hand finally reached for the small bottle and she smiled. "That's very kind of you, Mr. Harley. I thank you," she said delicately. She looked admiringly at the perfume, then opened the bottle, dabbed a little on her wrist and sniffed. Her pleased expression satisfied Jed.

Jed cleared his throat. "By the way, you never did say why you're going to California. What your plans are."

Dawn's eyes lowered to the table. She picked up the neatly folded cloth napkin set next to the plate and cutlery and began fiddling with it.

"You don't have to tell me if you'd rather not," Jed said.

With her eyes still down and her fingers busily creasing the smooth fabric she said softly: "I really don't have any plans. For the past couple years I've just been traveling in that direction. I guess the longest I've stayed in one place was six months. In Wyoming."

"No job?" Jed asked.

Dawn looked a little embarrassed. "I don't have one waiting, if that's what you mean. I was hoping to find something suitable in California."

Jed pondered for a moment. "Maybe it's not my place to be asking, but is it necessary for you to travel to California—to look for work, I mean?"

Dawn regarded him with a curious expression.

Jed shifted in his seat. "What I'm saying is, if it's a job you're looking for . . . I could use some help at the store."

"I'm not without means, Mr. Harley," Dawn stated formally. "And I'm not looking for any favors."

"You're misunderstanding my offer, Miss Prescott. It's *you* who would be doing me the favor."

Dawn sipped on the last of her tea, waiting for him to explain.

"I run the store on my own—since my father died," Jed told her. "I've been thinking of taking on some help but just never got around to it. And, if you pardon my saying so, I don't think an attractive face behind the counter would be bad for business."

Dawn felt herself blush. She blushed easily.

Instead of responding to Jed's offer, she asked casually: "Do you live here in the city?"

Jed knew she was stalling, and he truly didn't know why. His offer of a job was a genuine proposition—sort of. He needed a little extra help at the store and a pretty girl like Dawn certainly would attract the male clientele. But he also couldn't deny that he was not eager to see her leave Colfax. He knew that if she did there was little chance he would ever see her again. And that had become a painful realization.

He sighed and answered her question. "No. Got a little farm a few miles south of here."

Dawn blinked, but other than that her expression remained set, though she could scarcely imagine a man of Jed's apparent refinement working the land.

Jed could read into what she was thinking and so explained, "Most of my working day keeps me inside so I appreciate having a reason to spend time outdoors. Not as much as I'd like, though."

"Which is why you'd like to hire extra help at the store?" Dawn surmised.

"That's exactly right," Jed said, smiling.

Dawn also smiled, inwardly. "Looks like without my intending to I brought this conversation back to its start."

Jed lifted an eyebrow. "Except for providing me with an answer."

"I—I really don't know how to answer you, Mr. Harley," Dawn said, exhaling a soft puff of breath. "Your offer is most generous, but as I told you I do have other plans."

Jed leaned forward slightly in his chair and spoke to her straightly. "You could put those plans on hold for a while, Miss Prescott. California will always be waiting."

Dawn sat quietly with her thoughts for the next several minutes. The look on her face offered no clue as to what her decision would be. But then, with the faintest parting of her lips, she picked up the small bottle of perfume.

"I suppose I should give this back," she said. "Or at least pay you for it."

"No," Jed replied, crestfallen at what he perceived as her rejection.

She surprised him. "Then—I should accept it as an advance on my salary."

Jed shook his head, smiled and said tenderly, "No. Accept it as a gift."

And so Dawn did postpone her plans and went to work at the mercantile. It was pleasant enough and while the job didn't pay more than what she had earned at the hotel restaurant, she found her duties more stimulating and enjoyable than waitressing and dishwashing. What she quickly discovered was that although Jed had told her he'd wanted help so that he could spend more time working on his farm, he was at the store virtually every day, from opening to closing. But Dawn never questioned why that was because she liked working beside him. Jed was professional in managing the affairs of the store— efficient in dealing with customers and suppliers.

Efficient, yet never officious. Dawn found Jed a kind and thoughtful boss who was patient with her while she learned her myriad tasks. Soon she was not only serving customers but also purchasing items from salesmen and maintaining the inventory. It wasn't long before she knew almost as much about the business as Jed.

Much to her surprise, Dawn felt content living in Colfax. It began to feel like her home, the first real home she had known since leaving Montana. Through her work she quickly got to know many of the town's citizens and it was apparent they had begun to regard her as one of their own.

As did Jed. He often took her dining and when business was brisk, brought their meals to the store where they would eat in the back room between customers. One evening he treated her to the theater, where a traveling troupe from Boston performed. It didn't take long for Dawn to notice the attraction he had for her. And while she wasn't sure of her own feelings—unsure if she even *had* feelings beyond friendship for Jed —she never discouraged his thoughtful gestures.

On a slow Tuesday afternoon Jed decided to close up the mercantile early. He had rented a carriage from the livery stable and asked Dawn to take a ride with him out to his farm. At first Dawn was hesitant, and embarrassed with herself for being questioning of his intentions. But finally she did accept his invitation, reminding herself that during their time together Jed had never behaved as less than a gentleman.

Jed rode slowly so that Dawn could enjoy the countryside. It was a sunny May day and while the Nevada temperature was in the high eighties, the open road provided a refreshing cool breeze that whistled in from the north. Neither spoke much during the ride—Dawn shy and perhaps still a bit tentative; Jed preoccupied with what he was going to say once they got to farm—until at one point Dawn said wistfully: "I haven't rode in a carriage since I was a little girl."

Jed's eyes shifted toward her after her comment. Her expression was far off, vacant. He realized that he really didn't know anything about the girl's background. All she'd ever told him was that she was born in Montana. But she never spoke of her family and why she had decided to set out on her own. There was still that sadness in her eyes, however, that hinted at some past unhappiness.

The north road out of Colfax branched off into a winding trail, surrounded by mesquite, sagebrush, and sparse desert fauna. The trail entered onto Jed's property and ended at the picket fence surrounding the small wood-framed, white-trimmed house. Dawn was frankly surprised; she had expected to see a more rustic dwelling. But the house was quite charming, another reflection of Jed's good taste. When Dawn remarked how impressed she was, Jed proudly told her that he and his father had built the house themselves.

"My father was good with his hands." He added modestly: "Reckon I inherited some of his skill."

They sat in the carriage for a few more minutes while Jed surveyed his house and small parcel of land with a look of deep satisfaction. Dawn could tell how much he loved his property, and she couldn't help sharing his contentment.

Suddenly, a big, old dog appeared from behind the house. He slowly approached the closed gate, only his throaty grunts and wagging bushy tail giving show to his pleasure at seeing Jed.

"That's Husky," Jed said by way of introduction. "Been with me for a lot of years."

Dawn smiled at the dog. "Hello, Husky."

"He's a fine animal," Jed said with affection. But then he sighed. "He's getting on, though."

Jed helped Dawn down from the carriage and escorted the girl through the swinging gate into the yard. He took a moment to pet Husky before taking Dawn inside the house while the dog waited obediently out on the porch. The house seemed much larger inside, though the atmosphere was cozy, and the place immaculately kept. The wood fixtures were sturdy and meticulously polished and the seating arrangements richly upholstered and comfortable. A large Oriental rug covered most of the parlor floor.

"You and Husky live here alone?" Dawn asked as she glanced admiringly at the decor.

"Ever since my father died. My mother passed away some years ago. Actually we built this place as a kind of therapy. Hard work keeps the brain occupied."

"I—imagine you and your father were close," Dawn ventured, a slight halt in her voice.

Jed nodded. "We were. Very close. Especially after Mother died."

"I lost both of my parents," Dawn then offered.

Jed lowered his eyes in sympathy. "I'm sorry to hear that."

"You don't have to be sorry." Dawn managed a rueful smile. "You understand what it's like."

"I do. But . . . it's just that you're so young," Jed said, his face somber. "Listen, would you like to sit down? I can make us some coffee."

Dawn declined the offer of coffee but took a seat on the sofa. Jed sat himself on the chair across from her.

Dawn spoke pensively. "I was twelve when my father died. I guess my mother wasn't able to, as you say, keep her thoughts busy enough. She died just a short time later."

Jed let out a compassionate sigh. He asked: "Is that when you went off on your own?"

"Wasn't long after."

Jed decided not to ask her any more questions. Dawn's sad eyes had assumed a pained look as she reflected upon difficult memories. They sat in silence until Dawn returned from the distance of her thoughts. She regarded Jed with a self-conscious smile.

"I'm sorry," she said.

Jed brushed aside her apology. He politely asked her: "Would you mind if I came and sat beside you?"

"I don't mind."

Jed rose and stepped over to the sofa. He seated himself next to Dawn and tenderly took her hand, his fingers curling and lightly closing through her lithe, slender fingers. Dawn glanced down to the slow interlocking of their hands but did not resist or pull away.

"Miss Prescott," he said, using the formal address by which they continued to refer to each other, "as you can see, I have a fine home. I have a good livelihood. The only thing I'm missing is someone to share it with."

Dawn remained quiet, her body quite motionless. She raised her eyes toward him.

Jed looked directly into the softness of her eyes. "I can provide a good life . . . for a wife."

Dawn still didn't speak. The smile she wore was tentative.

Jed continued, "It doesn't seem right for two people to be alone—if they don't have to be.

What I'm saying, Miss Prescott, is . . . I'd be honored if you would agree to marry me." His tone was subdued and polite. The intention in his words strong and sincere.

Dawn flicked her eyes away from his, briefly . . . before returning to meet his gaze.

"Marry you?" she murmured.

"I know marriage is not in those plans you were talking about," Jed said. "And maybe I'm not the man you ever saw as a husband. But I confess that I've fallen in love with you. Actually, I've known it for quite some time."

Dawn searched for the right words with which to respond. "I haven't known a lot of men, Mr. Harley," she said. "But I don't think I could meet a finer man than you."

Jed leaned in a little closer beside her, respectful yet hopeful. "Then accept my proposal— Dawn. I'll never give you cause to regret your decision."

Dawn gave him a long, deep look. She felt bewildered as this had come upon her much too suddenly. She'd known that Jed had been attracted to her, but she truly never guessed the profoundness of his feelings.

And while outwardly, since her father's death, she had refused to acknowledge such a desire . . . inwardly Dawn sought security. The security that Jed Harley was now offering. She could not say that she loved him. That kind of love required a maturity that Dawn, despite her years of independence, had not yet reached. The only love with which she was familiar was the love she had felt toward her parents—especially her father. But from what she recognized was inside Jed, his kindness and compassion, she also believed it was possible that she could grow to have deeper feelings for him.

As if responding to a will outside herself, or perhaps it was that dormant longing, she accepted Jed's proposal. And then, for the first time in the months since he had come to know her, Jed asked her permission to kiss her. She agreed. He kissed her delicately, respectfully, with gentle affection, and as his lips touched her cheek a warm shiver rushed through Dawn.

Gradually, she did come to feel—perhaps not a true heartfelt love, but a strong caring for Jed. That he loved her, she had no doubt. He spoke the words every day, often several times throughout the day. And while it was more difficult for her to express in words what she felt, she responded to the love that he professed in ways that were more comfortable for her. By doing simple things that were showings of her affection.

Dawn settled into her life on the farm. She looked after Jed when he came home following a long day at the store. On occasion she would ride into Colfax with him and help out at the mercantile. Jed himself rode into town on his horse, but had purchased a carriage from a seller who had given him a good deal so that Dawn could ride to Colfax like a proper lady, and in comfort.

But mainly Dawn stayed at the house, cleaning and learning how to cook those meals that Jed particularly enjoyed. She would greet him on his return each day, Husky following behind, wagging his tail with as much enthusiasm as he could muster at his age. Dawn grew to love that old dog, who quickly became as much a loyal companion to her as to Jed, as if acknowledging his canine contentment at his master finally finding happiness.

After supper they would often bring Husky along and go for long walks in the nearing twilight, or perhaps sit out on the porch, holding hands, talking or just quietly enjoying each other's company, with the old dog stretched out at their feet. On Sundays after church Jed would do most of the work that needed to be done around the place and Dawn would frequently lend a hand, donning a battered, wide-brimmed Stetson to protect her fair-complected skin from the harshness of the Nevada sun. Life was busy but uncomplicated. Dawn often thought how this wasn't the future she had seen for herself when she'd set out from the wide open landscape of Montana, and occasionally when watching the glorious sunset over the western mountain range, she ruminated on what her life would have been like had she completed her journey to California. But Jed proved himself true to his word and Dawn was content.

They lived a quiet, simple but pleasant life . . . until the day three men on horseback rode up to the farm.

CHAPTER TWO

It was early evening, just before sunset. The western horizon was alive with colors; a majestic, natural display reflected off the snow-crested peaks of the Sierra Nevada.

Late autumn. The long months of winter were not far off. Jed was in the garden harvesting the vegetables when he saw the three riders approaching from the west. Two of the men rode erect, but Jed noticed that the third man seemed slumped on the saddle. Even though they were off in the distance, Jed didn't like the look of the men. He hoped they would just pass by without stopping.

But the men kept heading in the direction of the farm. Jed's eyes never left them as he walked from the garden toward the house. Dawn was in the kitchen preparing some of the fresh vegetables Jed had brought in earlier.

"Some riders approaching," Jed said to her calmly.

But Dawn could sense that Jed seemed concerned.

"Trouble?" she asked.

"Probably not," Jed replied with a reassuring smile. "But I think it best if you stay indoors until I find out what they want."

Dawn could understand Jed's caution. They lived several miles from town and had no close neighbors. They rarely received unannounced visitors, and those who did come by were generally townfolk with whom Jed was familiar. It was obvious that Jed did not recognize these people.

But what Jed did know and hadn't shared with Dawn was the news circulating around Colfax that remnants of the notorious Chancer Gang had been responsible for a recent stagecoach robbery just outside of Reno in which the armed guard was killed.

The Chancer Gang had established a fearful reputation throughout the Southwest, leaving a trail of blood and carnage across Texas, New Mexico, and Arizona. They had successfully eluded the authorities until earlier in the year a sheriffs posse out of Yuma had shot down leaders Bob and Jonas Chancer, along with several members of the gang in a bloody gunfight that also left two of the posse dead. It was undetermined how many of the outlaws escaped the ambush, but it was believed that the survivors had routed into California, heading north before holing up in the mountains of the Sierra Nevada. The men were desperate and dangerous and a hefty reward of two thousand dollars was offered for information that could lead to their capture.

Jed was a peaceful man who abhorred violence, and although he owned a gun, a preloaded Navy Colt single action percussion revolver, he never armed himself. His contention was that a gun was an invitation to trouble, as he'd witnessed during those lawless years in Colfax. The gun he owned was kept under lock in a drawer in the bureau. He briefly considered strapping on his holster before going outside, then decided against it as he did not want to unduly alarm his wife. Besides, he'd never had occasion to use the Colt and wasn't even sure if the weapon still fired.

He finally told himself that chances were slim these riders were the wanted desperados. More likely just passersby seeking directions.

Feeling a bit more confident, Jed stepped back outdoors. By now the riders were lined up on their mounts outside of the fence. Jed stayed put on the porch, close to the door.

"Afternoon," one of the riders greeted. He was sitting on a big sorrel. The other two men were riding bay roan geldings.

"Howdy," Jed returned pleasantly. "Anything I can do for you?"

"Was hopin' we'd meet with a friendly offer," the rider said with a grin, speaking in a deep, reasonant voice. "Truth is, we been ridin' for quite a spell and would surely welcome the chance to water our horses—if not ourselves."

Jed looked with a concerned frown at the man

who was slumped forward on his saddle. He appeared ill.

"Is your friend all right?" he brought himself to ask. "Looks like he might be sick."

"Oh, Jim here's just tired—and thirsty," the man on the sorrel replied amiably. "Like I said, we've come a long way."

Jed nodded and gave a quick study of each of the men. The "talker" was a tall man with a well-developed physique, about thirty, with hard-edged features, high cheekbones, and sallow skin. He had on a wide, black Stetson that he wore low, shading dark-circled, weary eyes. The other erect rider looked to be about the same age, but had a burly build and when he took off his hat to wipe his brow exposed a prematuring and patchy baldness. He had heavy-lidded, drooping eyes and wore a dull, lifeless expression, which likewise was yellow complected. The man slumped in his saddle had his head raised enough so that Jed could tell he was a dark-skinned Mexican. All of the men looked dirty and had several-days' growth of beard.

Jed also noted with some concern that each of the riders wore sidearms.

Whoever these men were, despite the "friendliness" of the one doing the talking, Jed felt uneasy in their presence and would have preferred them off his property. Still, he wasn't about to ask for trouble and so invited them to fill up their water canteens from the well at back of the house.

"What about our horses?" the balding, burly man asked in a blunt tone.

"There's a trough in back."

The talker leaned forward on his saddle and rested a black leather-gloved hand on the pommel. "That's might neighborly of you, friend. We'll bring our horses round."

Jed nodded. He stayed put as the riders slowly backed their mounts away from the fence and started for the rear of the house.

They never made it as suddenly the Mexican emitted a quite audible groan, stiffened in the saddle, then dropped sideways from his horse into the dirt. He lay motionless.

Jed instinctively started to come forward off the porch—only to have a gun drawn on him by the talker. A shiny, nickle-plated .44 Colt revolver was pointed in his direction.

"That's far enough," the talker said smoothly.

Jed halted as he felt his heart skip a beat.

The burly man climbed down from his horse and walked over to his fallen companion. He knelt beside the prone body, gave it a shove to no response, then looked over to his partner.

"He's dead," he said flatly.

"Yeah, I figgered," the talker said emotionlessly, raising his Stetson up over his brow with his free hand. "Surprised he lasted this long. Damn shame. Well, easier to divide by two than three. More profitable too. All right, take his saddle-bag, Sam. We'll leave our other gear with the horses. Then you and our friend here better bring Jim inside the house."

"My wife's inside—" Jed started to protest.

The talker clicked back the hammer on his revolver. "You really wanta argue with me?"

"Then—at least let me go inside and talk to her first," Jed implored.

"Not likely."

"Look, I don't intend to give you any trouble," Jed told him.

The talker grinned again, only this time his toothy smile had lost its benevolence. "No question of that. But can't never be too careful."

Jed knew that he had no choice but to go along with whatever they wanted. He turned his head toward the house and saw Dawn peering out through the parlor curtains. Her face was stricken; she'd seen everything.

The two men entered the yard and led Jed inside the house—the talker holding a gun, the burly man called Sam carrying the saddlebags over his shoulder. The talker then stayed inside with Dawn while Jed and Sam went back out to bring in the dead Mexican. They laid his body on the sofa while Dawn stood aside, her face blanched.

"He's been shot," Jed muttered to his wife.

"Yeh, hell of a thing," the talker said. "Got drunk last night and started to clean his gun. Didn't know the damn thing still had a charge in it. Blew himself a neat little hole in the side."

Sam's mouth twisted in a semblance of a smile. Neither Jed nor Dawn found amusement in the story. Or believed there was any truth to it.

"You'd better take the horses round back," the talker instructed his partner.

"You'll find no barn," Jed told him outright.

"As long as they're outta sight," the talker said without concern.

Jed stood next to Dawn, who nuzzled up close to him. He marshaled his courage and asked the talker: "What do you want here?"

The talker spoke easily. "Just lookin' for a place to lay low for a while."

"How long?" Jed demanded, trying to maintain at least an appearance of authority in front of his frightened wife.

"Don't rightly know. But we can make our stay a whole lot more pleasant if you two cooperate."

"I already told you, I won't give you any trouble."

"That's fine," the talker said. He cast a subtle glance at Dawn.

The girl tensed and averted her eyes sharply from a look she could not quite decipher. Then she turned her face fully toward her husband.

Jed wrapped an arm around her waist and gave her a reassuring squeeze.

"Since we're all gonna be like family for a while, figger I should introduce myself. Name's Walt Egan. My unmannered partner's Sam Bond." He jerked a thumb to the body on the sofa. "That *was* Jim Torres."

"The Chancer Gang," Jed muttered almost in a gasp.

"What's left of it," the man who called himself Walt conceded. "And you two might be . . ."

Jed felt a sick churning in the pit of his stomach. He suddenly realized that these men intended to kill them before they rode off. Walt Egan wouldn't have so freely offered their names otherwise. He only prayed that Dawn didn't share the same thought.

Jed's throat had gone dry, but he managed to say: "My name's Jed. Jed Harley. She's—this is Mrs. Harley."

Walt spoke directly to the girl. "Ain't you got no first name?"

"Dawn," she said, trying not to sound intimidated.

Walt nodded approvingly. "Might purty name —Dawn. Like the sunrise, eh?" He glanced around the house. "And a might purty place you got here. Yeh, think I'm gonna like it here just fine."

"For only a few days," Jed reminded.

Walt glared at him. "For as long as I say." He gestured with his nickle-plated revolver for the couple to go sit at the table in the kitchen. They complied . . . but before they could reach their chairs they heard a couple of feeble, throaty barks come from Husky in the backyard . . . followed by a single gunshot. A quick yelp. Then silence. Dawn's eyes widened reflexively and she stifled a gasp as Jed drew her closer.

And just moments later Sam Bond reentered the house. He'd reholstered his gun and was casually picking dirt from his fingernails with a small pocket knife. His face had no expression.

"Just done your dog a favor," he said to the couple. "That mangy old mutt wouldn'ta lived to see winter."

Dawn pressed into her husband. "Oh Jed . . ." She sobbed.

Jed spoke up. "You had no call to do that."

"No, he *didn't*," Walt said firmly, tossing a stern look to his partner.

Sam caught the disapproving look but ignored it with a shrug. Instead he said: "You picked a fine place, Walt. Don't look like no one's around for miles."

"Yeah," Walt replied absently. He hooked a thumb at the body on the sofa. "We'll have to do somethin' with Jim 'fore he stinks up the place."

"And what 'bout his horse?" Sam asked with a sudden glint in his eye. "Won't be needin' three of 'em, seein' that Jim won't be doin' no more ridin'."

Walt knew where he was headed. "Don't be gettin' no more ideas, Sam," he warned. "And that goes for the animals too. Damn, you're too eager for gunplay. I'll figger out somethin'. In the meantime just leave the horse with the others."

Sam grunted morosely. "Got 'em out back in the corral."

Walt stepped over to the parlor window and glanced outside. The sun was starting to set as the shadows grew long across the yard.

"It'll be dark soon," he said. "Sam, you and Jed here'll take Jim out and bury him. Find some spot that won't make it look like no grave. We don't wanta be leavin' signs that we was here." He said to Dawn, " 'Til then, you got somethin' to cover him with?"

Dawn looked to Jed for permission, who nodded. She went into the bedroom to get a blanket while Sam followed and stood outside the doorway, watching her. Dawn grabbed a quilt from the bed and turned for the door. She saw Sam blocking the entrance, leaning his heavy body against the door frame. He was looking at her from under his drooping eyelids. Dawn chilled; there seemed to be no life, no emotion in his eyes—just dark, empty pits. She veered her focus away from his stare and asked him politely yet firmly to let her get through. Sam still didn't move. It was as if he were toying with her.

"Sam, let the lady be," Walt's voice commanded from the parlor.

Sam complied, but rather than stepping aside he pushed his back against the doorjamb to let her squeeze by.

"Cover him up nice, lady," he said tonelessly, eyeing her with his vacant stare.

Walt said to his partner, "Since you're up, check round and see if Jed here has any dangerous weapons layin' about."

"I don't own a gun," Jed quickly replied.

Walt gave Jed an appraising look. "No, don't imagine someone like you would."

Jed's body coiled and he had to muster self-control not to call Egan on what he meant by his remark. They might be helpless under the out-laws' guns, but that didn't mean Jed had to put up with having his manhood called into question in front of his wife.

Sam gave the house a perfunctory search but could not find any guns—and not the one weapon that Jed did own, the Navy Colt, locked away in the bureau drawer. He then said he was hungry and demanded something to eat. Walt confessed that they hadn't eaten since yesterday and would appreciate some grub.

Jed nodded to his wife and Dawn went about preparing the outlaws the meal she had intended for Jed and herself. She had developed admirable cooking skills and always made a fine supper on Saturdays. Tonight she had cooked a chicken along with garden-picked vegetables and sour-dough biscuits. She served the men out of a sense of necessity, silently, with no enthusiasm. Walt Egan and Sam Bond devoured their food while she and Jed sat cuddled up to one another on the floor in the parlor. Sam suddenly demanded alcohol. Jed said that they didn't keep liquor in the house and his answer upset the thirsty outlaw. Walt finally interjected and said that coffee would be fine. Dawn got up to pour them each a cup, then went back to her husband.

After he and his partner were done gorging themselves, finishing off their meal with generous slices of the apple pie Dawn had baked for dessert, Walt invited the couple to have their own supper, but neither had the stomach to eat. The outlaws' presence and the dead body on the sofa had sufficiently taken away their appetite.

Sam thumped his chair away from the table and let out a belch. Walt at least had the courtesy to say: "That was a fine meal, Dawn." With his eyes still on the girl, he added: "You live well, Jed, I gotta tell you."

Jed was about to comment, but instead he clenched his jaw to keep his words in.

Walt spun around to Jed and said: "Well, it's dark enough for you two to get to work. You got a shovel, I reckon."

Jed didn't reply, but he started to get up from his place on the floor. Dawn held onto his arm firmly. Jed patted her hand and gently pulled away. "I'll be all right," he told her.

"Sure he will, Dawn," Walt said, though in a questionable tone.

Jed's eyes flashed angrily toward the outlaw and he spoke with intent. "I'm giving you fair warning, Egan. Leave my wife be."

"Jed, I take that as a plain insult, after all the hospitality you've shown us," Walt said, feigning offense at what he was insinuating.

"I won't be long." Jed smiled at Dawn. He paused. "And I'll—take care of Husky too."

Once the men went outside to do their task Walt invited Dawn to come sit with him at the kitchen table. Dawn icily ignored him and stayed seated on the floor against the far wall. Walt shrugged indifferently and began to roll himself a cigarette.

"You don't mind?" he said politely.

Dawn turned her head stiffly toward the window. But after only a few moments she brought herself to ask: "Why did you have to come *here*?" She spoke with barely concealed contempt for the outlaw.

Walt lighted his cigarette by striking a match against his thumbnail. He inhaled deeply and blew out a fine stream of smoke.

"Just your bad luck, I reckon."

Dawn kept her voice steady: "What *are* you planning to do with us?"

Walt turned his head and looked at her for a long while, puffing contentedly on his cigarette. His eyes seemed to lose some of their hardness.

"Don't be concernin' yourself over that."

"But—we know who you are."

Walt regarded the glowing tip of his cigarette. "So does the whole of the Southwest."

"You won't be leaving witnesses," Dawn said, tentativeness starting to edge into her voice.

"Often don't," Walt said casually.

Dawn was too preoccupied to determine whether Walt was serious or not.

"Then why should Jed and I be any different?" Dawn asked, struggling to maintain her courage. "You've killed before."

"Can't deny that I have," Walt admitted. "But only to protect myself." He took a pull on his cigarette. "Makes no matter, though. If they ever bring me in alive, I'm takin' a walk straight to the gallows. But I don't intend to swing at the end of a rope." He took a pause. "Saw a man hanged once," he said pensively. "Took him damn near twenty minutes to finally die. He just swung there, stranglin' and twitchin' on that rope. . . . Never forgot that." He went quiet before he switched back to topic. "But no, I ain't never shot a man just for the sport of killin'."

"What about—your friend?" Dawn asked,

meaning Sam Bond. "The way he just shot our dog. Any man that could do that . . ." She looked pained at the memory of that vile act.

"Sam's a mean one, I grant you. The worst kind: simple mean. He's got the killin' urge and it makes no difference if it's man or animal, woman or child. But he listens to what I tell him. I ain't a-scared of him and he knows it." Again Walt's voice took on a gentle tone. "Look, I don't want you to be worryin'."

And strangely, inexplicably, with just those few words, Dawn began to feel more at ease with the outlaw. She could see that he regarded her as a person and not just a hostage, a useful tool—or the object of some overt or even passive desire, which had been her initial fear. Even though she understood both she and Jed were his prisoners, she felt she could somehow trust him.

But she did still worry about the man called Sam Bond. He'd proven himself to be a mean, brutal type—now further confirmed by Walt. With Jed as helpless as she was, Dawn would have to rely on Walt to protect them.

Walt noticed that his coffee cup was empty. He raised it to Dawn. "Would you mind?"

And Dawn rose from the floor and walked over to the counter to fetch the coffeepot. She poured what was left into Walt's cup, half filling it, and her eyes leveled on the nickle-plated revolver lying next to him on the table.

"Gettin' ideas?" Walt asked only half-seriously as he caught her gaze.

Dawn smiled warily.

"It scare you?"

"I—don't like the look of guns," she admitted.

"Neither does your husband, I take it."

"Never knew any good to come from a gun," Dawn said.

Walt frowned. "Often not. 'Course, depends on how you use it."

"Hasn't done you much good," Dawn dared to say. She permitted herself to sit on the chair opposite Walt.

"Wouldn't necessarily agree," Walt said calmly, without offense, taking another pull from his cigarette before grinding it out on his dinner plate.

Dawn regarded him with an incredulous look. "How can you say that . . . when you've told me they're waiting to hang you?"

"It's the life I chose, Dawn," Walt replied matter of factly. "And I reckon outside of those men I was obliged to kill, I ain't got no regrets."

Dawn gave her head a slight bewildered shake. "How could anyone choose to live such a life?"

"Sometimes in that you don't got a choice," Walt said. "Without really aimin' to, you cross the line. Then you gotta decide which way to go." He exhaled reflectively. "But I reckon my path was set from the minute I was born. Always had to live by my own rules. Even as a kid."

"I suppose in some ways I was like that," Dawn offered mildly. "After my parents died. Maybe I still am."

Walt said: "Anyway, ain't nothin' I could change, even if I was so inclined."

"But the day's going to come . . . ," Dawn started to say.

Walt started building another cigarette. "Maybe. Probably, in fact. They sure ain't gonna go easy on me, like they did with Frank James. But I can't be concernin' myself over it. Hell, worry'll kill you faster'n a bullet."

All at once Dawn felt an odd sort of pity for the outlaw. He had chosen his path in life and seemed resigned to the almost certain consequences. She felt sad, and that emotion played on her face.

Walt noticed her look, and smiled.

"Your husband a good man?" he questioned. "Seems to care for you."

"He *is* a good man," Dawn stated. "And he *does* care for me."

"You love him?" Walt asked bluntly.

Dawn felt herself flush a little. She didn't answer his question quickly or directly. What she finally said was: "I told you . . . he's a good man."

Walt cocked a brow. "Hmmm," he sounded in

a curious way. Then he rolled his shoulders and said: "Well . . . if all goes well, we'll be ridin' out in a coupla days."

"They'll still be looking for you," Dawn reminded, unnecessarily.

"Have been for a long time." Walt grinned. "Haven't caught up with me yet."

Although Dawn did not voice it, she outright surprised herself with the thought: *And I hope they don't.*

Those few minutes with the outlaw seemed to reassure Dawn. She truly believed she could take him at his word—that no harm would come to her or Jed.

At least not from Walt. But she couldn't feel quite as confident about his partner.

Walt smiled crookedly. "Reckon I could go for another piece of that apple pie."

Dawn raised a faint smile back at Walt and cut him a slice.

Sometime later Jed and Sam Bond returned to the house. Both men were covered in flecks of dirt and Sam was breathing heavily from his labor. It was obvious to Dawn that despite his powerful build he wasn't used to manual work.

Jed had the glimmer of tears in his eyes, most likely for his beloved Husky. But he instantly changed expression and looked questioningly at his wife, to find her sitting at the table with Walt Egan, both appearing as casual and relaxed as if they were old friends sharing tea. He didn't know what to say . . . but Walt broke the momentary silence, reverting to his hard-edged tone.

"All taken care of?" he asked Sam.

"Yeh . . . an' the dog too," Sam said miserably.

Walt glanced toward Dawn, but his words were spoken to Sam. "Just wanta tell you agin: that was a mean, dirty thing you done, shootin' that animal."

Sam grunted and turned away.

Walt pulled out an open deck of playing cards from his shirt pocket and began shuffling them. He cast an eye over at Jed. "Up to playin' a hand of poker?" he asked.

Jed looked surprised at the cordial offer. "What about your partner?"

"Sam don't play cards. Me—I like to relax with a coupla hands."

Jed shook his head. "Sorry. Don't think I'm up to relaxing. And I—don't play cards, either," he said curtly.

Walt gave his own head a shake and regarded Jed with the twist of a smile—a smirk that said in effect: "Figured as much." Walt put the cards back into his pocket and stood up from the table.

"In that case, think we'd all better bed down. Sorry 'bout the arrangements, but Jed, you and Dawn'll have to sleep out here where we can keep an eye on you. You can decide which of you will take the sofa. I'll sit up first. Sam, take the bedroom, if you want."

Jed walked over to Dawn, still regarding her uncertainly. Dawn smiled at him and took his hand.

"It's all right, Jed," she said.

"Everything's fine," Walt piped in. "Your wife and me was just havin' a little talk, that's all." He added: "She's a fine woman, Jed."

Jed gave his head a wary nod.

Neither Jed nor Dawn could bring themself to sleep on the sofa. Not after a dead man had lain there. Both could not sleep in any case. The house was dark except for the faint light provided by the kerosene lamp kept aglow on the kitchen table. For the first part of the night Walt sat at the table, smoking, drinking coffee from the fresh pot that Dawn had brewed, and silently keeping watch. Sam Bond snored loudly from the bedroom, his choppy breathing disturbing the quiet that had settled upon the house. Finally, well after midnight, Walt got up and went to waken him for his shift. Jed and Dawn could hear Sam grumble and Dawn grew uneasy with him now taking over. She kept thinking how he had so viciously shot Husky . . . and what Walt had said about him having a "killing urge." He was a man to fear and she only prayed that if he should decide to provoke trouble that Walt was a light sleeper.

When Walt was in the next room and they had a few moments alone, Jed finally spoke to Dawn —in a whispered voice.

"What were you two talking about when I was gone?" he asked.

"He gave me his word that nothing would happen to us," Dawn replied.

Jed made it clear he wasn't convinced. "You're accepting the word of an outlaw? The man's a killer."

"Yes," Dawn said confidently. "I trust him."

"Musta been some talk you had," Jed said with a slight edge to his voice.

And before Dawn could respond, Jed rolled over onto his side, facing away from her.

They pretended to be asleep when both of the outlaws came out of the bedroom. They listened as Walt and Sam talked quietly between themselves and carefully emptied the contents of the saddlebags onto the kitchen table. They could hear them counting the take, the crisp sound of folding money flipping between their fingers and slapping onto the table like playing cards. While they couldn't make out much of what they were saying, as their words were mumbled, they suddenly heard Sam whoop: "Almost three thousand dollars!" Then Walt's voice raised just enough to tell him to keep his mouth shut.

Sam said, more quietly: "That makes my

share . . ." A long pause as he calculated. "Over a thousand bucks."

"We split evenly, Sam," Walt said, his voice equally muted. "But we don't go spendin' it too quick. This money is new-issue currency."

After the money was divided at about fifteen hundred dollars apiece it was returned to two of the saddlebags, which Walt insisted he take with him to the bedroom while Sam sat up for his watch.

Sam cursed under his breath, Walt again told him to shut up, and no more was said.

Dawn listened and thought with irony how there was no trust among criminals.

Morning arrived, announced by the muted glow of sunlight that streamed into the house through the light fabric of the drawn curtains.

Neither Jed nor Dawn knew what the new day, Sunday, would bring. But coupled with the uncertainty they both shared, Dawn soon became aware of a difference in Jed: a strange distance, one which she had never experienced from him in their almost fourteen months of marriage. She tried to convince herself that it was just the way he was handling their situation. Perhaps he felt inadequate in his role as protector. Embarrassed that his strength as a man had been compromised.

But she instinctively knew he felt threatened in another way: by the doubt that maybe something . . . personal had gone on between her and Walt Egan the night before.

Jed's strange attitude continued throughout the day, and it seemed to confirm Dawn's suspicion. Jed was a man possessed of the most basic values and she could sense his disapproval as Walt would engage her in friendly conversation while she went about her chores. Jed became withdrawn and sullen—and increasingly resentful at the intrusion the two outlaws had made upon their life.

And yet there was the truth that Dawn felt ashamed to acknowledge, if only to herself. The truth that she *was* attracted to Walt. The initial fear and contempt she'd held for the man had been released from her. Instead, the moments she now spent with him seemed to awaken and arouse something deep within her. Not physically, as there had been no such contact between them. It was more of a yearning, foreign to the world to which she had become accustomed since marrying Jed, encouraged by Walt's determined independence and his sense of adventure. His rugged individualism, which she found exciting to the point of giddiness—and so much at odds with the gentle if conventional nature of her husband.

She had come to realize that she too shared Walt's independent spirit. It had been a vital part of who she was ever since the day she ran off as a teenager from her guardians' care. An independence born of and nurtured by the death of her parents and the loss of her home. It marked the end of childhood innocence and the sense of protection and comfort that came with it. Yes . . . when she first met Jed she did want the security he offered. It was an emotionally fueled return to the past that had so suddenly and cruelly been snatched from her. But once settled into married life, was the contentedness, the happiness, really a facade? A mask so convincing that it fooled even herself. Yes . . . she could now admit that. She truly had herself believing that she enjoyed making a home for Jed and caring for his needs as a good wife should. But within her heart she knew that it was a stifling and unsatisfying existence. Through no fault of Jed's. He had done his best for her. She had simply been denying the person she really was. A denial that she accepted—until her inherent spirit was once again unleashed by the arrival of Walt Egan.

This realization forced Dawn to face her true feelings for Jed. And the reality saddened her. Because she knew the truth had come out when Walt had asked her that night at the kitchen table if she loved her husband.

Why did he ask her that? she wondered.

Why couldn't she simply have answered "Yes"? Instead, while the word played loosely in her brain, she could not speak it. She replied only that he was a good man. Which he was. Which he had been since the first day she had met him. But if she could not admit that she loved Jed, she could not have had the feelings for him that she had made herself believe she had.

Jed's odd, cold behavior since the arrival of the outlaws also made her question things about her husband. It was as if she were discovering a side of him she never knew existed, and one which she found distasteful. Perhaps his true nature, which he had also kept hidden.

As twilight approached and she walked in solitary thought around the property under the watchful eye of Sam Bond, Dawn reached the painful decision that she could not go on living the life she had. As much as it might hurt Jed, she could not maintain the pretense of happiness and continue masquerading a false truth—a lie that, if not now, would surely eventually prove even more hurtful and unfair to both Jed and herself.

The dilemma she faced was that she could not share Walt Egan's life either. An existence really that saw him forever on the run, with a tragic destiny already set. There was no turning back for Walt—he admitted it, and no matter how much she now knew she wanted to ride off with him when the time came, she could not envision a future as the companion of a wanted man.

No, that could never be, she told herself firmly.

65

And while she could not embrace the honesty of love, she did indulge herself to a brief, romantic fantasy of riding beside Walt and sharing his roaming and adventures. She recalled the play of muscle under the tightness of his dirty, flannel shirt, even when performing a gesture as simple as lifting a coffee cup, and flirted with how it would feel to be held in his strong arms.

She'd never lost the imagination of her youth, she thought with a heavy sigh.

On Monday Jed rode into Colfax to work at the mercantile, dressed sharply, as usual, in a dark suit and starched white shirt. It was Walt who insisted that Jed resume his workday ritual so that no one in town might grow suspicious if he failed to show up at the store. It was a safe move since Jed would never be so reckless to alert the law with his wife staying behind with Walt—and especially Sam. Jed had been hesitant to leave, and Dawn wondered if he feared less for her safety than her spending the day with Walt.

Shortly after finishing the hearty breakfast of flapjacks and crisp bacon that Dawn had prepared, Walt came outside and walked over to the girl as she stood by the split-rail fence surrounding the perimeter of the property, gazing into the west. It was a clear, crisp autumn morning and the air was invigorating. Walt took in a deep, deliberate breath, which he exhaled hard, calling attention to his approach. When Dawn turned to look at him her expression instantly registered surprise. His face was washed and shaved. She noticed for the first time how truly ruggedly handsome Walt was. His strong physique and broad shoulders such a contrast to Jed's pleasant but refined features and rather delicate build. And he walked with such confidence, a masculine gracefulness. She actually felt herself grow a little weak as she watched him come toward her.

Walt felt a tad self-conscious at her admiring stare. He rubbed the palm of his hand over his cheeks and down along his neck. "Borrowed your husband's shaving tools," he said.

"I'm sure he won't mind," Dawn lied.

"I asked him to keep his ears open round town," Walt said. "If things are quiet me and Sam'll be ridin' out tonight."

"Tonight?" Dawn echoed with a bit more emphasis than she'd intended.

Walt nodded. "Fact is, Dawn, it ain't a good idea to keep Sam cooped up in one place for long. He tends to get antsy. He's likely to do anythin' to kick up a little excitement."

Dawn took a few steps forward, returning her gaze to the distant mountains of the Sierra Nevada. "Where will you be going?" she asked.

Walt exhaled. "North probably. Like I told you, we got almost all of the Southwest lookin' for us."

Dawn spoke tentatively. "If you made it north . . . would you ever consider . . . maybe settling down?"

Walt flashed a quick, surprised look in response to what she was asking, then became thoughtful as he considered her question.

"I dunno, Dawn. Tempting thought, I suppose. But what else would I do? I don't know no other trade than robbin' banks and stages. And there's Sam . . ."

Dawn turned to him. Her voice took on a sudden forceful tone. "You don't owe anything to Sam. It's probably mostly because of him that the law's after you."

Walt dropped his head, amused by her comment.

"I'm serious." Dawn's eyes hooked into his and her voice was steady. "Maybe you had to shoot men in self-defense, but Sam's just a cold-blooded killer. You said so yourself."

Walt's expression became curious. He squinted. "What're you gettin' at, Dawn?"

Dawn gazed back toward the mountains cresting above the landscape. She thought for a moment how the mountains reminded her of Walt: tall, proud . . . mysterious. And they represented freedom. The freedom that Dawn believed in her heart they both could have.

"You probably got enough money in those saddlebags to make a new start for yourself," she said softly.

"Hardly."

Dawn hesitated for just a moment before adding: "What about Sam's share?"

Walt's face hardened. "You suggestin' I should double-cross him?"

"How do you know he's not thinking of doing the same to you?" Dawn challenged.

"Now you're talkin' foolish, Dawn. Me and Sam have rode together for a long time. Been through a lot together, and even though he's crazy as a bedbug I never once felt I couldn't trust him."

Dawn went silent. Then she said slyly: "I've noticed how you don't leave the saddlebags alone with him."

Walt raised his black Stetson up over his forehead. "Why're you talkin' this way, Dawn?" he asked seriously. There seemed to be more than mere curiosity in his voice. A suspicion, maybe.

Dawn realized that she might have said too much and offended Walt.

"I'm thinking of you, Walt," she explained as innocently as she could. "That maybe if you'd just ride away you could start a new life."

"Is that all?" Walt asked specifically.

Dawn hesitated, then she came out and spoke the truth. "Maybe *we* could start a new life."

Walt pulled off his Stetson and slapped it against his thigh. "Talkin' foolish, I said? Now you're talkin' just plain crazy."

Dawn made herself not to appear insulted by his words.

Walt grimaced. He spoke to her a trifle condescendingly. "Hell, Dawn, you're just a kid. And a married one at that. What—you plannin' just to up and leave your husband?"

Dawn didn't answer. She just kept looking at him, her eyes firm and steady.

"I thought you told me you loved him," Walt pressed.

"I *care* for him," Dawn corrected, mustering honesty in her voice. "I made myself believe I loved him . . . but I was just looking for something. Something I've found I don't really want."

"And when did you find that out?" Walt inquired, though already guessing the answer.

"When I met you," Dawn confessed.

Walt gave her a sideways smile. "Kinda sudden, ain't it?"

"What I feel toward you, maybe," Dawn conceded. "But not what I know about myself."

"And what's that?"

Dawn spoke with passion. "That I never should have made the decision to marry Jed. That I wasn't made for this kind of life."

"And you think the way I live is any better?" Walt asked subtly.

"But it doesn't have to be that way," Dawn argued. "We could go off and start a new life—a better life—together."

"Yeah, and once Sam found out I ran out on him, he'd come after us. Trust me, you wouldn't want that, not with Sam." Walt added solemnly: "And what 'bout Jed? You think he'd just let you leave?"

"I don't know," Dawn said with a sigh.

"Well, I do," Walt said straightly. "He'd set the law after us pronto. And I got enough hangin' over me without bein' accused of stealin' a man's wife. No, Dawn, you gotta stay where you belong . . . and I gotta do what I do. Each of us got a road to travel, though it maybe ain't what we want."

"I know what I want," Dawn murmured. "And that's to be with you."

Walt's voice was mellow. "Dawn, if things were different I'd be flattered to have a girl like you beside me. Reckon I feel that way now. But we gotta speak truthful. The life you're suggesting sounds fine, but it can't never be. Not for me. And I won't bring you into it."

Dawn didn't say anything more. She realized there was nothing she could say that would alter Walt's objections. But whether she rode off with Walt or not, she did make up her mind about one thing:

She was going to leave Jed.

Jed's mind was far removed from his work. He went through the motions of serving customers, but not with the enthusiasm with which he usually did business. His brain was a whirlwind of thoughts, mainly worry about what was going on at the house. He wasn't concerned for Dawn's safety. Sam Bond was a threat, but Walt Egan was in charge and could handle him. He wouldn't allow any harm to come to Dawn. But what Jed feared was that he couldn't trust Walt, either. He'd seen how he paid too much attention to his wife, which Jed also noticed Dawn didn't discourage. As hard as he tried, Jed couldn't ease the thought that there was something going on between them. And the longer Walt stayed at the house, the stronger the possibility that Jed could lose his wife to the dubious charms of the outlaw.

Mondays were generally slow days at the mercantile, and today wasn't any different. Shortly after 1 p.m., Jed decided to close up the store. After he locked up, he stood out on the street in front of his establishment and struggled with the only decision he believed he could make.

He had to notify the marshal, Henry Thornton.

It was a risky move, he knew. But if his gut instinct was correct, Walt Egan would not hurt his wife no matter what Jed did. And then he'd either be arrested—or shot—and both Jed and Dawn would be rid of his influence.

He finally made up his mind. He wanted Walt Egan off his property—and out of their lives.

Marshal Henry Thornton raised himself from his desk, focusing on Jed with a penetrating expression.

"You're sure it's them?" he asked.

Jed nodded. "Sure as I'm standing here talking to you."

"And Mrs. Harley is with them?"

"I already told you she was," Jed replied with impatience.

Marshal Thornton went to the gun rack at the other side of the office and withdrew a model '73 Winchester. He paused and then said thoughtfully: "It's too risky to ride out with a posse. Too many men would be sure to alert them. Be dangerous for your wife."

"Egan and Bond are too dangerous for any one man," Jed said.

Thornton regarded Jed with mild offense. He was forty years of age, in strong physical shape, and had been the marshal of Colfax for almost five years, with a good record of arrests to his credit. He was highly regarded by the citizenry.

"I'm a lawman, Harley," he said curtly.

"And they're desperate killers," Jed reminded unnecessarily.

"I know what they are," Thornton said. "I've read all the bulletins." He carried the Winchester back over to his desk and removed a box of .40–44 cartridges from the side drawer. Then he broke open the breach and began sliding shells into the chamber. He loaded the rifle to its fifteen-round capacity.

"You're not taking chances, are you?" Jed noted, impressed at the marshal's efficiency.

Thornton glanced up at him. "You want the truth? I don't expect to be bringin' 'em in alive."

"Fine with me," Jed said through pursed lips. He asked: "What about your deputy?"

Thornton shook his head. "Kid's too eager. Better if I leave him behind." After he was done loading the Winchester, he said: "We'll have to play this smart, Harley. By that I mean you'll have to do your part."

"I'll do whatever you suggest," Jed told him.

Thornton explained his plan. "I'll ride out with you partway, then I'll hold back. They'll probably check round once you come home. Now exactly at four o'clock, get 'em sittin' down to supper. They can't be by no window or any other place where they might see me getting' into position or it's game over." He locked his eyes hard on Jed. "Now comes your part. Findin' some way to get 'em both outside into the open where I can get a clean shot at 'em." He abruptly added: "If it comes to that."

Jed looked thoughtful—and suddenly a tad uncertain. "That shouldn't be . . . too difficult."

The marshal seemed oblivious to his hesitation. "Good. But as I told you, I'm aimin' on a good, clean shot—if need be—and it gets dark early this time of year. That doesn't give you a lot of time. And if Mrs. Harley stays indoors, one or the other might decide not to leave her alone. I need 'em both outside together. She might have no choice but to come out with 'em."

"You a good marksman?" Jed asked carefully.

"Yup," Thornton answered. "By the way, Harley. You own a gun?"

Jed nodded. "Keep it locked in a drawer. I've never used it."

Thornton considered for a moment. "Maybe that's for the best," he said.

Jed got back to his little farm shortly before three. Marshal Thornton rode with him but stayed back about a quarter mile from the property. As Thornton had predicted, Sam Bond came outside once Jed rode up and, without uttering a word, frisked him. He checked around the property, and then stepped outside the yard and scanned each direction into the distance. Jed so wanted to get away from him that he didn't bother to unsaddle his horse after he got it into the corral.

When Jed walked inside the house he saw what he'd expected—and dreaded. Dawn was in the kitchen preparing the evening meal and Walt was sitting at the table watching her with a cigarette dangling from his mouth while cleaning his nickle-plated revolver by running a patch wetted with oil down the barrel then through each of the six chambers. Six bullets were laid out on the table before him. Dawn had obviously provided him with the cleaning supplies and Jed doubted that Walt had to use much persuasion. Jed's jaw clenched but he maintained his composure. Ignoring Walt, he walked over to his wife and planted a gentle kiss on her cheek. She responded with a tentative smile.

"You're home early," Dawn said, though with scarce enthusiasm in her voice.

"Slow at the store. Typical Monday," Jed replied perfunctorily, noting her uncommon demeanor. "Everything okay here?"

"Fine."

"Be eating soon?" Jed asked, trying to sound casual. He could feel Walt's cold eyes watching him. There was a palpable tension in the house. He could feel it emanating not just from Walt, but also from Dawn.

Dawn nodded. "In about an hour."

Jed glanced idly at the clock sitting on the fireplace mantel in the parlor. The timing for supper looked right for what the marshal was planning. He poured himself a cup of coffee and moved into the parlor, Walt's stare following him.

Walt finally asked: "Hear any talk in town?"

Jed merely shook his head.

"None of your customers say anythin'?"

"No," Jed replied tersely.

"Reckon that could be," Walt said, though his tone was a little dubious.

Sam Bond strode inside. He looked at Walt and nodded his head, telling his partner that Jed had come back alone.

Shortly after four, they all sat down to eat. Jed tried to pretend that he had an appetite, but he wasn't hungry. Dawn had made a fine meal of spareribs, potatoes, and vegetables, along with buttered biscuits. Walt and Sam both dug into their food, but Dawn ate as little as Jed. No one spoke, though Jed would catch Dawn averting her eyes when he would periodically look over at her. He did notice the quick, furtive glances she cast toward Walt. He could feel his body growing taut with repressed rage, but he had to stay relaxed. He kept reminding himself that it would all be over soon.

His concern now was how what was going to happen would affect his relationship with Dawn. She'd know it was he who had gone for the marshal. If she did possess feelings for the outlaw Walt, she may never forgive him. But dammit, he was her husband and he had every right to protect her. She might not look at it that way, though, and instead believe that he suspected her of what he did indeed suspect, and that through his action he had betrayed *her*. And if that did happen, he would have to face the realization that she had never loved him as he had believed—or hoped—she had. That he had been naive to her true feelings throughout their marriage.

Maybe he'd never been man enough for her. Perhaps Walt Egan represented the masculinity she sought in a male. The only way Jed possibly could have proven himself otherwise was by taking it upon himself to challenge Walt and his partner.

If only he'd had the chance. If only he had the courage.

Supper was finished and Jed rose from the table to take another look at the time: 4:43. Walt noticed him looking at the clock on the mantel.

"You got some special interest in the time?" Walt asked.

Jed turned to him, maintaining an innocuous, uncomprehending expression.

"Forget it," Walt said, raising a grin.

Jed knew he had to remain calm and steady. Walt was cagey; he'd be sure to catch on to any false move or hint of apprehension on his part. His main concern was to find some way to get him and Sam outside without arousing their suspicion.

Jed took a seat in the parlor and waited about ten minutes, nursing a cup of coffee, and then he said:

"Egan, I'd like to talk to you . . . and Sam." He kept his voice level.

Walt threw an arm over the back of his chair. "Go ahead, talk."

"Outside. I'd—prefer if what I have to say is said away from my wife."

Walt glanced at Sam and smiled enigmatically. "Oh."

Dawn regarded her husband with quiet suspicion.

"Reckon we could use a little air, walk off some of that fine meal," Walt said agreeably.

He stretched and started to rise from his seat. "Tell you what, though. I'd feel a mite more comfortable if Dawn came outside and waited for us on the porch."

Jed glanced over at his wife, who was looking at Walt.

"You okay with that?" Walt asked Jed, who nodded. Then Walt glanced at Dawn, who regarded him with a doubtful expression.

"Must be somethin' important you gotta be sayin' to us," Walt said as he holstered his nickle-plated .44 Colt revolver.

Jed swallowed and tried not to look at the gun. "It is."

Walt bit his lower lip. "Uh-huh."

The men started for the door. Dawn, however, stayed where she was, looking uneasy.

Then she spoke abruptly. "Don't do it, Walt."

79

Jed's eyes darted in the direction of his wife. Walt's head also twisted slightly toward her.

Dawn pushed out a breath and tightened her jaw. "Jed's up to something," she said.

Walt turned to Jed.

"Dawn . . . what—what are you saying?" Jed said, scarcely believing what he was hearing—*from his wife.*

"She right, Jed?" Walt asked, his voice tinged with a sinister inflection.

"Of course not," Jed replied quickly. "I—I just wanta have a talk with you, like I said."

Walt penetrated him with cobalt cold eyes.

Jed's own eyes were shifting. "Look, this is ridiculous. There's nothing I can do to either of you. And—and Sam saw that I came back alone." His nerves started to fray as both outlaws glared at him, their faces malevolent masks.

Jed spun around to his wife, perspiration beading his brow. "Dawn, what are you trying to do?"

"You *told* me what you want to do," she said in a cold, distant voice unfamiliar to her husband. "You told me last night how you planned to take the money and find a way to get rid of Walt and Sam." The words had come unexpectedly, without premeditation, as if she'd been compelled to speak them by some force beyond herself. Oh God, she didn't want to turn against Jed! All she knew was that she suddenly didn't trust him and that she had to protect Walt.

Jed was in utter disbelief, and was almost pleading. "You're talking crazy, Dawn! You know you are! Tell them you're wrong! For God's sake, *tell them!*"

Dawn just stood there, motionless, her face pale, her features devoid of expression. She looked numb, beyond reason or comprehension. Jed felt completely helpless.

"I don't think she is, Jed," Walt said with a threatening calm. Jed's sweaty, edgy behavior convinced him that something was up. But he didn't believe Dawn's claim that Jed was after their money. If Jed had set them up for an ambush it was for another, more personal reason. And Walt also knew that Dawn's betrayal of her husband was for a personal reason.

Sam Bond was a brute, a creature of pure instinct. The only understanding of which he was capable was survival. A survival he now saw threatened. His right hand moved reflexively toward his gunbelt, swiftly withdrawing one of his two Colt revolvers and aiming the weapon point-blank at the now-quavering Jed.

Jed's heart leaped into his throat. He panicked and made a dash for the door. Before Walt could stop his partner, Sam fired a single shot into Jed's back, and he crumpled to the floor. Dawn was jerked back to the moment by the report of the gun, and she shrieked in response, before settling her eyes on the fallen form of her husband.

Walt ran to the window and peered through the corner of the glass to see if the gunshot had alerted anyone who might be waiting outside. Sure enough he saw a man slowly raise his head from behind a thick clump of sagebrush out beyond the fenced in yard.

"See anyone?" Sam asked.

"Yeah," Walt muttered. "Seems Mrs. Harley was right."

Sam turned slowly toward Dawn. His yellow teeth were bared. "Yeh, and she knowed also," he said balefully. "She and that Jed were in it together. She just got scairt."

"Shut up, Sam," Walt barked. "She just saved our skin." He squinted out the window. "Don't know how we're gonna get by whoever's out there, though. Might just be the one, but can't be sure."

Dawn quickly recovered from her shock. She pulled herself together because she knew she could not give in to weakness. She had to stand firm for Walt, prove herself to him, and with that as her purpose she found strength in her voice.

"It's the marshal, probably. Let me handle it, Walt."

"You?" Walt said incredulously.

Dawn rocked her head once, but determinedly. "I can go out and maybe get him to show himself."

Walt bit down on his lower lip as he considered her offer briefly. Then he gave his head a nod. "All right, Dawn. Don't like it, but can't think of no other way 'less we shoot it out. But dammit, be careful."

Dawn allowed a moment to brace herself before moving toward the door. Another moment and then she swung the door open and rushed out onto the porch, her arms waving wildly, her voice panicked.

"Hurry! Please hurry! My husband shot one of them and has the other at gunpoint. Please help us!"

Walt watched her convincing display and was impressed. "Damn, she's good," he muttered to himself.

A voice called out from behind the sagebrush: "Are you all right, Mrs. Harley?"

"Yes," Dawn responded excitedly. "But Jed won't be able to hold him much longer. Please hurry! He needs help!"

And Marshal Henry Thornton, having no reason not to trust the pleadings of the terrified woman, rose from his cover and moved toward the yard, his Winchester cocked and at the ready.

As Thornton entered through the front gate and neared the house he said cautiously, "Move away from the door, Mrs. Harley."

Dawn did as she was told. Thornton carefully

studied her and determined that her anxiety was genuine. He stepped closer toward the house—

Suddenly Sam Bond swung around in the open doorway, grinning through yellowed and broken teeth and assuming a wide-legged stance, both of his revolvers drawn.

Thornton had only a split second to react. His rifle was raised and cocked and he managed to get off a single shot. Sam instantly fired both guns, slamming three bullets into his chest that sent the marshal sprawling backward onto the ground.

Sam's eyes went crazed and danced about in their drooping, heavy-lidded sockets, eagerly scouting to see if there were any other men for him to take down. But no one else appeared.

Walt stepped outside and observed his partner's handiwork. Even from where he was standing he could tell that the marshal was dead. Sam still had a wild look to him, but as he turned to Walt his expression slowly shifted to a masklike countenance of shock and surprise. His eyes dropped to his midsection and Walt's gaze followed. Sam's gut was gushing blood. His eyes were now wide as he raised them back to Walt. He started to say something, then collapsed in a heap on the porch.

Walt knelt beside him, turning him over onto his back. He looked helplessly at his partner's pale, twitching face.

"Looks bad, Sam," was all he could say.

"I—don't wanta die this way," Sam gasped. His body was squirming, his hands pressed tight against the wound in his belly as if to stop the flow of blood.

Walt understood. He slowly stood upright and ejected his nickle plated Colt revolver from his holster.

"Just know I'da wanted you to do the same to me," Walt said as he aimed the barrel of the gun at Sam's head.

Dawn turned her head away and just seconds later she heard the single gunshot, followed by a muted final groan escaping Sam's lips. Then stillness and quiet. She didn't look to see that Walt had mercifully ended what might have been a prolonged suffering for Sam with a well-placed bullet to the brain.

Walt stared blankly at Sam's body for several moments. Then he turned to Dawn, whose face was ashen. But with the brutal Sam now dead, she also felt a sense of relief.

"I hadda do it," was all Walt could say.

He and Dawn went back into the house, where they sat quietly for several minutes. Walt smoked a cigarette and recovered, but he now wore a look of concern.

"Reckon you got to make a choice," he said to the girl.

"I've already made my decision," Dawn said

firmly. She glanced at Jed lying still on the floor. And she felt strangely empty. The violence seemed to have drained all the emotion from her.

Walt sighed resignedly. "Can't say I'm in favor of it, Dawn. Gave you my reasons. But I owe you. And if you stay behind they're gonna have questions that you might not be able to answer."

Walt got up from his chair and walked over to Dawn and clasped her arms. She could feel the strength generated by his grip.

"You gotta be sure this is what you want," he said, looking deep into her eyes. " 'Cause the minute you ride off with me there won't be no turnin' back. And likely to be a rough road ahead."

Dawn spoke with confidence. "We'll make it, Walt. I know we will."

CHAPTER THREE

They saddled up two of the horses that the out-laws had rode in on. Dawn was given the mount that had belonged to the dead Mexican, Jim Torres, since Walt felt it would handle better for her. As Dawn climbed up on the horse, assisted by Walt, she was grateful that she had insisted Jed teach her to ride. Before departing, Walt had suggested that she try to find herself appropriate riding attire and Dawn selected one of Jed's weekend work outfits: an old flannel shirt and gray trousers. She felt numb as she put on the clothes worn by her dead husband. Clothing she had admired seeing him in as it had represented the most masculine side of his otherwise sensitive nature. Finally she capped her head with the wide-brimmed Stetson she'd worn to protect her fair skin from the sun when working outside with Jed.

Dawn walked out of the room and saw that while she was getting dressed Walt had dragged both Sam and the dead marshal into the house, leaving them lying on their backs on the floor against the far wall. But he had placed Jed's body comfortably on the sofa. Dawn gathered by the dismissive look on Walt's face that he neither expected nor wanted her appreciation. He merely shrugged and said that he had to fix things right.

But he didn't have her fooled. Dawn knew that he had indeed positioned Jed that way in consideration of her.

Walt didn't want to leave Sam's horse behind as a clue to their having been there, so he removed the saddle and Sam's other gear and gave the animal a sharp slap on the rump to send it off. As the horse raced free of the corral into the countryside, Walt carried the gear into the woodshed and hid it as best he could.

He reckoned they would have a good head start unless the marshal had informed anyone in Colfax of where he was going. Jed would eventually be missed at the store, but Dawn said it was doubtful that anyone would ride out to the farm for maybe a couple of days.

Since it would be dark soon, they only rode a few miles before setting up camp in a clearing among some underbrush. Walt collected some dry branches and brush and built a fire that warmed them against the chill of the late autumn night. Dawn had brought extra blankets from the house along with some coffee and a small supply of food that would sustain them until they could reach a safe destination to rest and restock before continuing their journey north.

As they sat across from each other close to the crackling fire, Walt observed Dawn carefully.

He finally spoke what had been on his mind.

"You know damn well Jed never said nothin' 'bout takin' our money."

Dawn was momentarily taken aback by his comment and did not reply. She didn't have to, though Walt's tone left it unclear whether he was grateful to Dawn for her actions back at the farm—or suspicious of her motives.

Walt had to be suspicious. It was how he lived. How he had survived. And Dawn acknowledged to herself that perhaps she had given Walt ample reason to doubt her. By her turning against her husband . . . and maybe he was also remembering her suggestion about running off with Sam's share of the money.

"I—just spoke what I felt I had to," Dawn said hesitantly.

Walt gave his head a neutral nod. "But you musta known what Sam would do, thinkin' that?"

Dawn sipped at the tin cup of coffee that she held tightly in both hands, as if to warm them. Her face was shadowed under the brim her Stetson. "No, I didn't figure on that," she said somberly. Then she gave her head a determined shake and spoke adamantly. "No, that's the one thing you have to believe. I didn't want to see that happen to Jed."

Walt squinted and questioned further. "And how did you know he'd bring the marshal?"

"I didn't," Dawn said firmly. "But I knew Jed long enough to see that he wasn't acting right. I . . . knew he was up to something."

"Yeah." Walt rose to his haunches and began to idly stoke the fire. "I reckon maybe Jed suspected somethin' more," he said, casting Dawn a sideways glance.

Dawn raised her face full toward him, her voice silent, though her thoughts were not quiet. She pondered Walt's remark. *Had he?* she wondered. Had Jed really thought "something more"? At first Dawn believed that to be true; it made her betrayal of Jed easier to deal with. It eased her guilt over those feelings she had developed toward Walt. But what if she *had* been wrong? Maybe that had been the farthest thing from Jed's mind. Yet how could that really matter now? Jed was dead. That part of her life was forever over. She still felt a little regretful over her actions, and their consequences, but she was not overwhelmed with guilt. She was where she wanted to be—with Walt.

She knew Walt was testing her. Determining his trust in her. She understood and could even respect that. As uncomfortable as it was for her, she sensed that all he wanted from her was her honesty.

"I'm not sure," she finally answered. "I'm not sure what he thought."

Walt breathed out hard. "Y'see Dawn, the thing

is I don't know how I feel 'bout that. I've only known you for a few days. Knowed Sam a whole lot longer, and I'll tell yuh: You was right. I never completely trusted him. That's why I did keep those saddlebags with me, like you noticed. Well, maybe it wasn't that I didn't trust Sam so much . . . it's more me just bein' the way I am. Just naturally careful."

Walt ceased talking. He concentrated on poking at the campfire with a long stick. The flames leaped up, accompanied by a flurry of glowing orange sparks. The splashes of light cast strange, maleovolent shadows across Walt's face. It was suddenly an eerie reminder of that which Dawn did not want to contemplate. The violence in Walt's past—and of which he might still be capable. She felt a momentary unease.

"Maybe you'd just better go on with what you're saying?" she suggested, speaking over a slight lump in her throat.

Walt sat back away from the fire, his face restored to the relaxed look with which Dawn felt more comfortable.

He built a cigarette, lighted it and exhaled a smooth plume of smoke. "You got me outta a tough spot. Woulda walked right into a bullet if it hadn't been for your suspicion 'bout Jed. But for whatever reason you did it . . . and whether you loved your husband or not . . . it's hard for me not to be thinkin' how you turned on him."

"I did it for *you*, Walt," Dawn said with emphasis.

Walt cocked his head. "Yeah, maybe you did. Nice to think that. But I got my own neck to be worryin' 'bout."

"I never loved Jed," Dawn finally admitted. "And even if I thought I did . . . it was never real."

When Walt didn't respond, Dawn finally voiced what he was obviously thinking. "You don't know if you can trust me."

Walt smiled crookedly. "If you was in my place . . . would you?"

Dawn looked downcast. "I thought when you brought me along with you . . . the things you said . . ."

"And I meant 'em," Walt jumped in quickly. "I want to trust you, Dawn. But how can I be sure? There's a reward on my head. You could live mighty well off that money."

Dawn took quick offense at what he was suggesting. "I never once thought about money . . . for myself."

"And maybe that's true," Walt acknowledged. "But after ridin' with me for a while, seein' what my life is really like, you might get to changin' your mind."

"No," Dawn said adamantly. "Not if we make it north like we talked about and use that money to build a new life."

"And what if we don't get that far?" Walt queried carefully.

"We will." And Dawn spoke her two words with such conviction that she almost had Walt convinced.

"Maybe we can head into Canada," she suggested. "No one would be looking for you up there."

"That's a long winter's ride." Walt sighed. "Unsafe country too. 'Specially for a woman. What I'm sayin' is, if we chose that road, our troubles ain't even started yet."

"How far north could we go?" Dawn asked.

Walt blew out smoke from his cigarette, then tossed what was left into the fire, watching it spark. "Depends," he answered. "Even ridin' with Sam, that's a rough journey. Ridin' with someone who's unfamiliar with what's ahead . . . well, that's a downright risky proposition."

"Maybe—it would have been better if I'd stayed behind," Dawn said contritely.

"No Dawn, we both know you couldn'ta done that," Walt offered solemnly. His voice grew soft and persuasive as he added what he knew Dawn wanted him to say: "And if it makes you feel better . . . maybe after a bit I could come to trust you."

Dawn's eyes fell upon him, hopefully.

Walt explained: "Reckon I couldn't feel no other way, seein' how you're willin' to make that kind of a ride with me."

"I am," she told him earnestly.

Walt then shook his head, deliberately. "Wouldn't consider no travel like that 'til come spring."

"Then where would we go?" Dawn asked with concern.

"East. Head into Utah," Walt said. "Know a fella who has a place there. Used to ride with his son. Kind of a strange old cuss, but I'll hand him a few dollars and he'll look after us for the winter. It's pretty remote and I'm not as well known there. Yeah, we should be all right."

The sky was clear after the mounting cloud cover moved west and the stars were twinkling brightly. Under different circumstances it could have been a perfect night. In some ways, to Dawn, it was. An unexpected shiver raced through her body, and it wasn't from the night chill. It came from inside her; the delicious sensation she got just from being with Walt. His mere presence stimulated every nerve in her body. She'd wanted him in a way she never wanted Jed. . . .

She knew it was wrong. Jed's body wasn't cold yet and she was inundated with improper thoughts toward another man. Not love, but an overwhelming passion. It was something over which she quickly discovered she had little control. It was also a desire she could not admit to Walt. Because she could not guess whether Walt shared what she felt. He wasn't a man open to revealing his emotions. Although she'd expressed her want to be with him and confessed her true feelings regarding Jed, he'd offered her nothing in return. If she spoke up now he'd probably think either she was a silly little fool or was disrespectful to the memory of her husband. And so she would have to wait. Until she knew where she stood with him, until she could be sure he trusted her, Dawn decided to maintain a distance and keep her thoughts carefully guarded.

"Gonna be a cold night," Walt said as he observed her responding to the shiver. "I'll sit up and keep the fire goin'."

Dawn looked at him and said gently: "Isn't there another way for us to keep warm?"

Walt instantly regarded her with a startled, if slightly mischievous expression. A look that Dawn had not deliberately intended to provoke.

"Mr. Egan, I assure you I'm not suggesting anything more than sharing our body warmth," Dawn explained, adopting a dignified manner.

. . . Though she wondered if Walt suspected that her outward formality did not reflect her inward desire. She yearned to have the strength of his big body next to hers.

"Oh, I wasn't thinkin' that you were," Walt replied quickly, if not necessarily honestly, raising both hands in a defensive gesture. "But I gotta sit up anyway and keep watch. Maybe I'll try and catch some shut eye later."

"I can take over when you're ready for some sleep," Dawn offered.

Walt rose and patted imaginery sparks from the campfire off his shirt. "One of us gotta."

Dawn looked up at him through her lashes. "You trust me?" she asked cautiously.

Walt smiled crookedly. "Reckon I'll find out. 'Sides, I've learned to sleep with one eye open."

Dawn opened her bedroll, laid out the blankets, and snuggled herself in. She tried to get some sleep but couldn't—though she pretended to. She feigned being asleep well enough to leave Walt wondering how she could drift off so quickly after all that had happened that day. Then he remembered how she hadn't displayed an ounce of sorrow or even remorse over her husband's killing. Not so much as a tear. Truthfully, he couldn't quite figure her.

But then, he'd rarely met a woman whose mind he could fathom.

The several days' ride they had hoped to complete was jeopardized when the very next morning a visitor showed up at the farmhouse. It was a business appointment that Jed had arranged the week before with a local builder named Jack Walden, who was going to provide an estimate for a small barn Jed was planning to construct on his property come spring. Walden wasn't alarmed when no one answered his knock on the door; he knew that Jed would be at the mercantile, and perhaps his wife was with him. Walden had agreed to ride into Colfax later and provide Jed with the figures. It was only when he happened to glance down at the wood planking of the porch and noticed a stain of what appeared to be blood that he became concerned. He decided to look around the property and came across more dried blood on the ground just a few yards from the house.

He walked back onto the porch, knocked again, then tentatively twisted the doorknob. The door was unlocked. He steadied himself as he made the choice to venture inside. He wasn't a brave man but he wasn't a fool, either. He didn't carry a sidearm and so instead reached for the bowie knife he kept in the sheath on his belt, and held it at the ready.

The house was quiet—and closed up. It was quite cold inside, as if a fire hadn't been lit to warm the house the night before. There was a faint, unpleasant odor present that he didn't immediately recognize. Before he could identify it, he discovered its source, emanating from the front parlor.

Two men lay dead on their backs against the far wall, visible gunshot wounds to their upper bodies. Walden immediately noticed that one of the men was Marshal Henry Thornton. Walden gasped involuntarily and started to step backward, reflexively tightening his grip on the bowie knife.

Then his eyes shifted and he saw Jed Harley stretched out on the sofa. Walden couldn't detect any injury, couldn't tell at first if he was dead or unconscious. But there was blood under him, staining the expensive fabric. Walden paled and forced himself to move closer to the sofa.

He was startled when a groan emerged from Jed Harley's lips. . . .

CHAPTER FOUR

Jed was alive, if barely. He was unconscious and breathing so faintly that Jack Walden had to check him several times to make sure that he really wasn't dead. It was only when Walden took his pulse and felt a weak throbbing in his wrist that he rushed outside, leaped upon his horse, and rode like the wind into town.

Things happened quickly. Walden explained the situation to Deputy Blackie Collins, who got him to fetch the doctor, Hiram Speer, and then told him to head back to the farm pronto to see if anything could be done for Jed Harley. Collins would round up some able bodied men as backup and follow presently.

Blackie Collins had served as deputy under Marshal Henry Thornton for not quite a year, assuming the position after Thornton's former deputy, a seasoned lawman named Curtis, was seriously injured after being thrown from his horse during a pursuit. Collins was young, in his midtwenties, and highly ambitious. He had been frustrated by what he saw as a prolonged apprenticeship, handling duties—chores really—that mostly offered no more challenge than keeping watch of the jail. His primary tasks in that regard consisted of bringing meals to the prisoners from the hotel and cleaning out the cells after a rowdy drunk had gotten sick during his stay. He craved adventure, which was why he gave up ranch work to become a lawman, but had not experienced much by way of excitement, outside of handling citizens' disputes or breaking up the occasional saloon brawl. While he never complained about the dullness of his work and carried out his humiliating duties with the modicum of efficiency each required, inwardly he resented Marshal Thornton for his apparent lack of confidence in his abilities. As Collins saw it, Thornton reaped the glory while he mopped up puke.

But now word was that the marshal was dead and, temporarily at least, he was in charge. He quickly recognized that whatever had gone on at Jed Harley's place could provide him with the chance to prove himself—and possibly convince the council to appoint him as the new marshal of Colfax. It was the opportunity he had been waiting for.

This was important to Collins as he once more was reminded of how little authority he held among the townfolk when he rushed into the saloon, the only place he could think of that would have a congregation of men present, and tried to gather up a few of the sober patrons to ride with him. No one took his request for volunteers seriously. In fact, he was downright ignored. It was only when he announced that Marshal Thornton had been killed and Jed Harley apparently wounded that he got a response. But it seemed to Collins that curiosity more than a sense of responsibility was the motivation of the five men who agreed to saddle up and go with him to the farm.

The men weren't sworn in as a posse. Collins didn't have the authority and Judge Reynolds was currently presiding over a legal matter in court. And as yet there wasn't the need to form a posse since it wasn't clear what the situation was at the Harley place. Collins only hoped that Jed was still alive and would live long enough to give him the details.

When they arrived at the farm and dismounted, Collins had the men wait outdoors and keep watch while he went into the house. The doctor was kneeling beside the sofa, his medical kit at his side, examining Jed, who was turned onto his side, the back of his shirt ripped open, with his bullet wound exposed. Doc Speer's face was set and serious. Jack Walden was also there, sitting at the kitchen table. Collins jerked a thumb to indicate for Walden to go outside with the others. Walden gave Collins an offended look but complied.

Towels covered the faces of the two men on the floor. Without saying a word to the doctor, Collins walked over to the bodies. He recognized the motionless form of Marshal Thornton and could tell from the severity of his chest wounds that he was dead. Collins didn't bother to remove the towel from his face. He felt no emotion other than suppressing a quick leap of excitement at this confirmation that he'd taken a crucial step in his career advancement.

He stepped over Thornton and knelt beside the second body, which likewise displayed no sign of life, and pulled off the towel. He felt a catch in his throat as he stared at the waxen face with the bullet hole in the forehead: the sightless, heavy-lidded eyes open and the mouth twisted in a grimace that reflected the shock of his death. Collins knew who the man was—or had been. He'd seen his picture on the Wanted posters that had been issued to the marshal's office. One of the faces he'd scrupulously studied during his idle times supervising the jail. Sam Bond—a member of the infamous Chancer Gang.

Collins dropped the towel back over Sam's face and pulled himself to his full height. He didn't announce his recognition of the outlaw to the doctor. He just asked about Jed's condition.

Doc Speer glanced over his shoulder at the deputy. He was an elderly, silver-haired man whose tired face displayed much of what he'd seen during a lengthy medical career, spent mainly in practices throughout lawless towns of the Southwest where violent death was common-place. But when he shook his head in reply to Collins' question, it was a gesture not of hopeless-ness, but almost astonishment.

"I don't know how he's survived," was all he said.

"You sayin' he'll live?" Collins asked with a lift of his brow.

"No, I'm not saying that," the doctor returned firmly. "In fact, I'm certain he won't. But I'd estimate he was shot sometime yesterday. How he made it through the night until now . . ." He shook his head again.

"Well . . . is there *anything* you can do for him?" Collins said, impatience starting to creep into his voice.

"Not here. He'd have to be gotten to town for immediate surgery. And in his condition I don't think he'd survive the ride. He's lost too much blood and it looks as if the bullet may have damaged his spine." The doctor sighed and spoke with little encouragement. "Even if by some miracle he pulled through . . . he'd be a cripple the rest of his life."

Collins moved over to the sofa and tightened his lips as he looked at Jed, lying pale and unconscious and as near to death as he'd ever seen a man.

"Any chance he might revive long enough to answer some questions?" he asked shortly.

Doc Speer excused the bluntness of Collins' question; after all, he was a lawman and had a job to do. But his concern was for the welfare of his patient, however limited that was. He replied thoughtfully: "No way of knowing."

Collins gathered a breath. "The way I figger it, if he's gonna die anyway, why not take the gamble and move him into town?"

The doctor gave Collins a critical look. "No gamble involved. It's a sure bet the ride would kill him."

Collins briefly contemplated the only two options available. If they let Jed be, there was a slim chance he might come around and give him the needed information before he expired. If they transported him into town it was the doctor's opinion he would surely die and then Collins would learn nothing. When he finally made up his mind, his decision was based on practicality. Compassion, if any existed in the deputy, was not even considered.

He said: "Doc, I'll follow your advice. We'll let him die here. But I gotta ask you if there's any way you can bring him around—just long enough for him to give us some answers."

The doctor looked exasperated. "Collins, I can't guarantee that. Even if he should regain consciousness, it's likely he wouldn't be able to tell you what you want to know. With the trauma and blood loss . . . why, I guarantee he'd be incoherent. That is, if he had the strength to speak at all."

Collins chafed at the old fool not giving him the respect he believed was his due: referring to him solely by his surname. He was also becoming frustrated. His only clue to what happened here was the body of the outlaw Sam Bond. But what he needed to know was whether any others had been involved—perhaps members of his old gang. That seemed highly probable since in the reports Collins had read Sam Bond was described as a psychopathic simpleton not known to ride alone. And if that was the case, there was a good chance his companions were still in the territory. This was a golden opportunity that Collins could not afford to let slip away.

He exhaled hard and said abruptly: "Well, any-thing you can do. In the meantime, I'm goin' to check round outside."

Before the deputy could leave Doc Speer made a throat-clearing sound. Collins halted, then looked back at him.

"I'd suggest you do something about—" The doctor tilted his head towards the two dead men.

Collins gave him a quick, annoyed nod. "I'll—send in a coupla the men."

Once the deputy stepped outside into the shade of the porch overhang one of the men walked over to him.

"We found only the one horse," he told Collins. "In back. Belongs to Jed. 'Least it's Jed Harley's name branded on the saddle."

"Belonged," Collins corrected hastily.

"Huh?" the man said with a puzzled expression.

"Jed Harley's not long for this world," Collins reported forthright.

Collins assumed a stance of authority, his legs spread apart, both feet planted firmly on the wood planking of the porch. He raised his voice to address all of the men. "And the marshal is dead . . . and so is Sam Bond, one of the Chancer Gang."

"Sam Bond killed the marshal?" one of the men spoke up excitedly.

"Either Bond . . . or one of the bunch he rides with," Collins offered. "We know 'bout the stage-coach robbery they pulled near Reno. They're in the state—or were, long enough to . . . do this. Witnesses from the stage holdup say there were three men. The report the marshal got from Reno says they were positively identified as Sam Bond and Walt Egan. Third was a Mexican. So it's likely to assume these men were here together."

"Why would Henry Thornton be out here alone, *Deputy?*" one of the men asked with a cocked eyebrow and an accusing edge to his voice.

Collins' face grew taut at what he was insinuating. "I knew nothing 'bout any of this 'til Jack

Walden came into the marshal's office this morning. Don't know what Marshal Thornton's reasoning was for comin' out alone."

"Well, didn't you wonder where he'd gone or why he didn't show up at the office today?"

"Marshal Thornton didn't always share his duties with me," Collins said curtly. "He had his own way of doin' things."

Another man said: "And what 'bout Jed Harley's wife? You find her in there?"

"His wife?" Collins echoed uncertainly.

"Sure," the man said with a smirk. "You didn't know Jed up and married 'bout a year ago? Where you been, Deputy?"

There was a smattering of laughter from the men that Collins knew was directed at what they perceived as his lack of experience. Though he ignored their snickers, pretended not to hear, it made him uncomfortable—and raised his ire. What made it worse was that they were ridiculing him over inconsequential matters and decisions made by the marshal of which he had not been informed.

But this reaction only fueled his determination to make each of these men—and the entire city of Colfax—come to respect him the way they had Henry Thornton.

Collins clenched and unclenched his jaw. "Whether or not I knew that Jed Harley had married ain't what's important," he stated formally. "And to answer your question: We only found the three men inside."

"Well, she ain't at the mercantile," a man offered. "Store's been closed all day."

"Then we have to assume that Mrs. Harley has been taken hostage."

"Yeh. Either that—or she's dead."

"Let's hope agin that," Collins said somberly.

"Can't Jed tell us nothin'?"

"Doc Speer has assured me that Jed Harley is dying. At the moment he's . . . not able to talk." Collins paused. "But I think we know enough to form a posse and get after these killers 'fore they leave the territory. I'm gonna ride back into town and get Judge Reynolds to swear in as many men as I can round up."

Suddenly there was a murmur of approval from the few men assembled.

"You can count us in," one chimed in.

"Good." Collins nodded with satisfaction. "In the meantime I'll need a coupla you men to stay behind—to help out Doc Speer with the bodies."

"Fine with Marshal Thornton—and Jed, if need be. But whyn't we just leave Sam Bond for the buzzards?" one of the men suggested without humor.

CHAPTER FIVE

Walt Egan woke with a start. His sleep heavy eyes roamed the campsite until they fell upon Dawn, smiling at him while she brewed coffee over a small fire she'd proudly built herself.

"Wha—What time is it?" Walt demanded as he scrambled out from his bedroll. "Why didn't you wake me?" He looked up at the clear blue skies. He felt the midday heat warm against his body. "It's gotta be damn near afternoon."

"You needed sleep," Dawn explained pleasantly. "I wasn't going to wake you until I knew you were well rested."

"Yeh, well, I'll be 'well rested' all right, if'n the law catches up with me," Walt grumbled.

Dawn poured a cup of coffee that she handed to Walt. "You didn't get to sleep 'til almost daybreak. You couldn't put in a full day's ride."

Walt's expression twisted sourly. "Ain't gonna put in no full day's ride now anyways."

Walt slopped down some of the coffee and looked closely at Dawn. There were noticeable circles under her eyes. Although she tried to conceal it with a cheery disposition, Dawn looked tired.

"And how much sleep did *you* get?" he asked.

"Enough," Dawn lied. She'd dozed a few times

during Walt's watch, but hadn't accumulated more than a half hour's sleep.

Walt spoke out the side of his mouth. "Surprised you slept at all, if you wanta know the truth."

"Actually . . . I didn't," Dawn then admitted.

Walt halted his drinking. He slowly pulled the tin cup away from his lips and looked hard at the girl. "And how are *you* gonna get through the day's ride?"

"I'll manage," Dawn replied simply, unconcerned.

Walt erupted. "That's just the kinda thing I meant 'bout you slowin' me down. We ain't even hardly started yet and that's twice you've messed up. Listen, I can get by with just a couple hours shut-eye. I'm used to it. But you . . . you're used to a comfortable bed and fine linens."

Dawn just kept smiling, unaffected by Walt's rant.

"I'm sure no one's come by the house yet," she said calmly. "If anyone does, it won't probably be 'til nightfall. No one's going to be all that concerned that Jed didn't show up at the store. He's missed days before."

Walt swept what was left of his coffee aside. He pointed a stiff finger at her. "You think that's all, huh? That's the least of my worries, if'n you wanta know. I ain't even bein' looked at for what happened there. I got Nevada trackin' me for that stagecoach holdup—not to mention four other states all armed with warrants that come outta the barrel of a six-shooter."

And with that Dawn's smile instantly dissolved, like moisture under the blaze of the desert sun. She knew that Walt was right. The truth she perhaps had tried not to acknowledge walloped her with the impact of a round of buckshot. He was a wanted fugitive with a price on his head, which many people were eager to collect. She realized that in trying to be considerate she may, in fact, have put him in jeopardy.

She lowered her head ashamedly. And almost at once Walt felt guilty for laying into her so roughly. Her sad, doe like chestnut eyes became even more sorrowful, and even to a man as hardened as Walt Egan what they reflected was heartbreaking.

Still, he wasn't a man easy with an apology. "I— I'm sorry if I upset you, Dawn," he stumbled. "Didn't mean to . . . to sound so ornery. But, damn, girl, you gotta know the seriousness of what you got yourself into."

Dawn's lips puckered. "I'm not upset at *you,* Walt," she said lowly, consumed with self-reproachment. "I deserve you getting angry with me. I'm upset with myself for not considering what's best for you."

"I know you was just bein' thoughtful," Walt said with a passive sigh. "And under other circumstances I'd 'preciate that. But 'til we reach Utah, it's gotta be all business. No time for carin' for what I might need—sleep, rest, eatin' right, whatever. Reckon that'll have to go for you, as well."

Dawn responded with an understanding nod.

Walt stood up and went to check the horses. Dawn started to clean up camp.

"We'll have to fill up the canteens once we come to some water," Walt said as he slid on his tight black riding gloves. "We'll likely have a long, dry stretch ahead of us after a few miles."

They were ready to ride within fifteen minutes. Both Walt and Dawn tried to clear the site of any signs that they had camped there, kicking and scattering about the burned remnants of their fire and other telltale debris. But even with their efforts it would be obvious to a vigilant eye that a campfire had been made at that spot.

As they started their day's ride, heading northeast on their long journey to the Utah border, Dawn struggled not to give in to the fatigue that had gradually taken hold of her. She tried to initiate conversation with Walt to keep herself alert, but Walt was quiet; perhaps, she thought, still angry at her for her carelessness.

Upon hearing the news of Marshall Thornton's killing, about twenty-five determined men showed up with Deputy Blackie Collins at the courthouse to be sworn in as a posse. Collins had explained the situation to Judge Reynolds and emphasized the importance of time in tracking down the outlaws, especially since it seemed likely that Jed Harley's wife had been taken as a hostage. The judge gave his official approval, despite Collins' inexperience. Both men agreed that riding with such a large number of men might not be wise given the heated emotion over the killings, and so Collins personally selected a dozen of the most able—and trustworthy. Still, before the men took their oath Judge Reynolds called for quiet and imparted his own stern words.

"I know how you men feel about what happened to Sheriff Thornton. He served our town well and he'll get a fine funeral. But I want to make it clear to each of you that you haven't formed a lynch mob. You've sworn an oath to pursue this matter with respect for the law. Now, if you meet with resistance, by all means protect yourselves. But if these men should surrender without aggression, I expect them to be brought into town in safety to stand trial. I can promise you that proper justice will be served. We also have to consider that Mrs. Harley may be a prisoner, and her life must not be endangered. Deputy Collins is in charge," he added, looking straight at Collins. "He'll be the one responsible to see that these instructions are carried out. I expect each of you to cooperate fully with him. If any of you feel that you can't abide by the law, if you're eager for 'frontier justice,' I'd appreciate if you would say so now. Because if there is any breach in these orders, not only you but Deputy Collins will stand accountable for it."

No one spoke up.

After the men were sworn in Judge Reynolds walked over to the deputy and put a hand on his shoulder.

"Collins, you've taken on a big responsibility," he said. "I hope you're up to it."

Collins nodded confidently.

The judge offered an incentive. "Bring 'em in and I'll personally recommend to the council that you be given the marshal's job."

"I'll bring 'em in," Collins said soberly, though inwardly he was about to bust a gut at hearing the words he'd been waiting for.

The judge added: "By the way, I'll be wiring Reno explaining what happened. I'm sure Sheriff Tyler is leading his own men, after that stage robbery. Chances are you may run into them. But as far as this posse is concerned, you're in charge. Any lead as to where these criminals might be headed?"

Collins thought out his answer carefully. "No lead. But I'm guessin' they'll travel east." He elaborated: "Wouldn't chance headin' back west after pulling that Reno job. Same goes for south. Every chicken farmer with a scattergun'll be lookin' for 'em, hopin' to claim that reward. And I don't figger if they've got a hostage they'll trek on north with the snows a-comin'. Too slow and it'd be too easy to track 'em. They'll head toward the east canyons, that's where I'd lay my money."

The judge seemed enormously impressed. "That's sound logic, Collins."

Just as Collins was about to exit the courtroom a man rushed in from the corridor to say that Doc Speer and two of the townsmen had just rode up.

"Looks like they might've brought in Jed," the man added.

Collins and the judge, followed by the men of the posse, stepped outside onto the steps of the courthouse. The bodies of Sheriff Thornton and Sam Bond were slung over the saddles of the townsmen's horses. Doc Speer had his own cargo in back of his wagon, covered with a blanket. He climbed off and walked toward the courthouse.

"Got Jed in back," the doctor said solemnly, sucking on a pipe. "He's dead."

Collins nodded impassively.

"Just so you should know," the doctor went on, speaking directly to the deputy, "he did come around—briefly."

Collins looked at him with anticipation.

Doc Speer formed his words around his pipe. "He spoke a few words. Gave a name you might be interested in: Walt Egan."

"Egan," Collins muttered, accompanied by anxious sounds from the men who formed the posse.

Collins told them all to quiet down. He next asked the doctor: "Is that all he said?"

Doc Speer shook his head. He withdrew the pipe from his mouth and, lifting and curving his leg, tapped out the ashes against the heel of his shoe. "No. As I expected, he was in a delirium, so make of it what you will. But just before he expired, he cried out, 'It was Dawn.'"

The doctor then lowered his head, turned, and walked back to his wagon.

"Dawn?" Collins said puzzedly.

"*Mrs.* Harley," one of the men informed him brusquely.

Collins turned toward the judge, whose face was set in a concerned frown.

"Don't know what he could have meant by that, Collins. But you make sure to bring Mrs. Harley in," Judge Reynolds ordered. "Let's find out what really went on there."

The autumn afternoon sun blazed hot as they rode across the sagebrush flat, and it was with shared relief when they came upon a lone cotton-wood set upon a grassy knoll. Its wide, leafy expanse offered welcome shade and Walt shifted his direction as he prepared to stop and cool the horses for a spell. Dawn was grateful for the chance to dismount, to stretch her legs and lift her rump from the saddle. They'd only rode for about three hours but it was the longest Dawn had ever been upon a horse, and she felt it. She was plumb saddle sore. Walt cast her sideway glances while he watered the horses. She didn't catch his eyes shifting toward her as she performed comical contortions with her body or as she massaged the circulation back into her aching buttocks. Nor did she notice Walt's amused expression.

Finally he took sympathy on her. "We'll go just a few more miles and set up an early camp."

Dawn was determined for Walt to know she was prepared to tough it out and declared that she would go on for as long as he felt necessary. Walt appreciated her offer but was not necessarily convinced of her fortitude. When he told her flatly just a few more miles, he could see the relief creep across her face.

It was another silent ride, their distance passing to the rear, the sun an orange ball just beginning to sink into the purple horizon beyond the western mountain ridges of the Sierra Nevada. Finally, Walt pulled his mount alongside Dawn and he turned to her with a grim expression set upon his features.

He spoke solemnly. "Dawn, I want you to make me a promise. If the law should catch up with us . . . I want you to tell 'em I took you as a hostage. Ain't gonna make no difference for me, but it'll spare you some grief."

Dawn looked back at Walt with a surprised

look, a sudden widening of her doe like eyes. She started to speak but Walt raised a gloved hand to halt her.

"It's the right thing to do," he went on. "No matter what you tell 'em, I'm gonna swing—or rather, that's what they got in mind for me. 'Course, I ain't never goin' out that way. But I ain't never gonna die easy knowin' they put you in a jail cell. So's what I'm askin' . . . is really for both of us."

"It'd be like I was betraying you," Dawn muttered, troubled at the thought.

She shuddered. For just an instant she flashed back to Jed—of what she had done to him. She hastened to erase that memory from her mind. It was still just a blur, one that she mercifully could hardly recollect. She still didn't fully understand why she had so cruelly turned against him. Still, she had spoken the words that had killed her husband.

She vowed that she would never turn against Walt—no matter what he asked.

"I need you to promise me, Dawn," Walt said, interrupting her thoughts.

She knew what Walt wanted to hear her say. What he *needed* to know. He was adamant about that and would accept no other answer. And while it was a lie down to the deepest part of her heart, she said quietly:

"I promise."

Walt looked closely at her. Despite the apparent

sincerity of her words, her eyes told another story. Walt instantly knew that he couldn't believe her. It saddened him because that meant he now had to make a harsh decision, one he'd been considering since that morning. For her own sake . . . come nightfall, when she was asleep, he would ride off alone.

They set up their second night of camp nestled beside a rock edged embankment near a clear, gently running stream. The location provided both clean drinking water and adequate cover. But lighting a fire would surely betray their position to anyone tracking them, and Walt was forced to be more cautious this night than he was the night previous. His main concern was that they'd made nowhere near the distance he had hoped they would today. By tomorrow it was imperative that he reach the protection of Rooster Canyon.

After he watered the horses he fed them some oats, then tethered both animals to the low hanging but sturdy branches of a dead tree. Dawn started unloading their supplies.

"Dawn, we're gonna have to eat and sleep cold tonight," Walt said as he squatted by the stream to scoop up and splash some water on his face and replenish the canteens. "Can't chance a fire."

Dawn shrugged and smiled and began rustling around inside the sack that contained the food-stuff. "There's some cold chicken. Or I can open a couple cans of beans. Got some biscuits." She glanced up at him, her eyes lowering, then raising. "And . . . the blankets and bedrolls should keep us warm enough without a fire."

Walt had to admit he admired her endurance. She hadn't uttered a single word of complaint throughout their ride. He could almost believe that she was prepared to stick it out with him, regardless of whatever difficulties they may encounter.

But it still made no difference to what he'd already decided.

Walt tried a different approach. Maybe by enforcing the realities they were likely to face he'd coax her into thinking twice about going on with him. Dammit, she was so brave about it all he didn't feel right about just riding off and leaving her cold.

"Still got a long ride to Utah," he remarked, creasing his brow and dragging the words out for emphasis. "We gotta get through some pretty rough territory. Long days in the desert, then there's the mountains ahead of us. The canyon trails can be pretty rough. Also, probably won't be the last night we gotta spend like this. Fightin' agin the cold. In fact, it's sure to get a whole lot worse."

Dawn was not dissuaded. She merely smiled without so much as a twinge of concern and replied: "Probably."

And with that simple word Dawn had unwittingly settled the matter for Walt—though not in the way he would have preferred.

They ate their supper of cold beans from a can and each munched on a piece of chicken. They sat close to each other under the warmth of a blanket. The late autumn skies were getting dark and there was no fire to provide light. Just the rising of the moon and the bright overhang of stars. It was a quiet meal until Walt spoke. What he said was strange—and perhaps uncharacteristic, given the type of man he was.

"Want you to know I 'preciate all you've done."

Dawn responded with a pleased expression, suspecting nothing deeper in what he was saying. His words were sincere and sounded innocent enough. Nothing to arouse suspicion in her as to what Walt was planning.

Walt cast his eyes downward. " 'Course I ain't happy 'bout the way things turned out. I mean 'bout Jed."

"That wasn't your fault," Dawn told him gently.

Walt was thoughtful as he picked at the canned beans with his fork. "Depends how you look at it. We hadn't come ridin' up to your place, none of this woulda happened."

Dawn lowered her lashes. "Suppose not. But—if you hadn't, I'd still be there . . . pretending."

"Reckon I feel sorry 'bout that also."

Dawn turned her face toward Walt and was wearing a wondering expression. "That's what I can't figure out about you, Walt Egan. You live the kind of rough life you do . . . and yet I don't think you're really that kind of person."

Walt appeared both surprised and amused at her assessment of his character. "You don't think so?" he said, adopting a hard tone.

Dawn shook her head with conviction. "You hide it pretty well, but you've got a side to you that's . . . well, not how you like to come across."

Walt grinned a little self-consciously. "I can name you at least a few dozen people who'd argue against that."

"People who've never really gotten to know you," Dawn inferred.

Walt was pensive for a moment, absorbing her words as if he'd never before considered that possibility. Finally he said: "Might have a point." And then he joked: "Try usin' that as a defense to a jury, though."

They fell into silence as night steadily encroached upon them. Once again the skies were clear and cloudless and vast, and the stars that pinpricked the veil of black blinked brightly. The moon rose above the horizon, suspended overhead like a silver disk. The temperature would drop considerably throughout the night but for now the air felt just right, its caressing cool providing a comfortable reprieve from the unseasonably scorching midday heat. The quiet and stillness surrounding their little refuge was palpable: pleasant and expansive, stretching for miles, only occasionally disturbed by the distant call of a foraging night creature.

And then, for the first time since she'd ridden off with Walt, Dawn became consumed by a strange but potent apprehension. She couldn't understand why this feeling had come over her, as she'd been enjoying a pleasant thought, picturing in her mind how perfect it could be if Walt could stop running just now and they could claim this peaceful solitude without threat. Perhaps that was what prompted her sudden despair. The rude return to a reality that was far removed from the crystalline tranquility of her imaginings. She sadly acknowledged that she had only allowed herself a brief respite from their situation. For as long as Walt remained on the run, fighting to stay ahead of the law, there would always be a danger traveling with them.

Fortunately, the anxiety gradually passed and she cleansed herself with a deep sigh that caught Walt's attention. He looked at her, curious, and Dawn just smiled timidly and resisted the urge to snuggle her body into his.

A few moments later, Walt said to Dawn: "You're a fine girl, Dawn."

"Fine *woman*," Dawn corrected playfully.

"Fine woman," Walt conceded.

Dawn's doe like eyes sparkled in the fading light. She spoke with a resolve intended as much for herself as her companion. "And we'll make a fine life together, Walt."

Walt did not acknowledge her comment. He pretended not to hear. As much as it pained him, he knew that the life Dawn envisioned for them could never be. Truthfully, he'd known it all along. Maybe Dawn did too, though she'd wanted to believe in the dream so strongly he couldn't disappoint her with brutal honesty.

At least he hoped she knew the reality. Because when she awoke later to find him gone, she would have to know that he had done it for her own good.

"Whyn't you try and get some shut-eye," he suggested. "Plan to put in a long day of ridin' tomorrow. Wanta be up come sunup."

"All right," Dawn agreed. "So long as you promise to wake me so you can get some rest."

Walt nodded.

Now it was Dawn's turn to be insistent. "Promise?"

"Sure," he drawled.

Dawn snuggled herself comfortably into the warmth of her bedroll. She was more tired than she would admit and knew that once she closed her eyes she'd be out until Walt awakened her. Walt moved close beside her and sat himself on one of the many large rocks that bordered the gentle currents of the stream. He sat so close to her, in fact, that Dawn could hear each of his breaths as he inhaled and exhaled in a slow, deep rhythm. The steadiness of his breathing comforted her. Dawn felt so safe and protected that within minutes she settled into the first good sleep she'd had since that fateful day when Walt came into her life.

Walt pulled out his tobacco pouch and rolling papers and began to build a cigarette. He lighted it by striking a wood match against the heel of his boot. He inhaled deeply, consuming the cigarette quickly. He then indulged himself to another smoke, all the while keeping an eye on Dawn over the dim light provided by the glowing tip. Soon he was listening to her faint snores. He knew it wouldn't take her long to fall into a deep sleep. She'd worn the look of exhaustion all day. He sucked the last bit from his cigarette and flicked what was left far into the distance, watching with interest as it sparked a faint path against the night skies before dropping from sight. Like a shooting star, momentarily flashing a cosmic trail before disappearing forever. While not a man given to profound thought, he recognized the significance and nodded his head in silent acknowledgment.

It was time to gear up his horse and start on his way. Guilt would ride with him, but he understood that even that would pass.

No, he thought as he untethered then quietly mounted his horse, he'd never met a girl quite like Dawn.

And he doubted he ever would again. . . .

CHAPTER SIX

Dawn slept soundly through the night, warmed against the cold by the added cover of blankets stretched over her bedroll. As she slowly started to awaken she felt relaxed and well rested. It was the sleep she'd needed. She had no reason to think that anything was amiss. But upon opening her eyes to the bright sunshine she gradually began to grow apprehensive. Walt hadn't wakened her and sunup, their departure time, had apparently long passed. She pulled herself free of the blankets and her eyes darted about the site. The small supply of food that they had brought along still remained . . . but she noticed only the one horse still tethered to the dead tree.

Walt was gone.

Dawn climbed to her feet and stood motionlessly, feeling instantly alone. She tried to convince herself that maybe Walt had just gone to fetch something for their ride, but she knew instinctively that wasn't so. For reasons she didn't know, he had decided to go off on his own.

Dawn fought against tears. She could not understand why he would bring her along this far and then just desert her. Her mind became a jumble of thoughts, trying to figure out his motive . . . but she couldn't come up with an answer. It simply did not occur to her that his riding off was to save her misery. All she knew was that she felt abandoned.

There was no point in trying to follow him. She knew he had rode off sometime during the night while she was fast asleep, and was certainly miles away by now. And she couldn't even be sure what direction he took. Maybe his telling her that he was riding to Utah was never his true plan. And even if it were, there was nothing she could do. She didn't know the country.

Confused and with a heavy heart, Dawn made the only decision she could: to turn around and head back home. And once there . . . she did not know . . .

As she climbed up on her horse and started the long ride back she determined that no matter what, she would not betray Walt. There would be questions concerning the killings of her husband and the marshal, and she would have to provide convincing answers. She would have to follow Walt's advice and claim that she was taken as a hostage—but she would not accuse Walt. She would say that she didn't know who the man was and that she had either managed to escape or was let go once her captor felt he had taken her far enough.

She rehearsed her story over and over in her head until she had herself convinced of its truth. They would have to believe her. Her one genuine worry was that she did not know what awaited her at the farm. It was entirely possible that the killings may have been discovered and that the law had already been at the house. With this playing on her mind, Dawn made the decision not to go to the farm. She understood that for her act to be convincing she would have to ride directly into town to report what had happened. She would have to call upon the same emotion she had summoned that had led Marshall Thornton into Sam Bond's bullet.

She hadn't ridden far before she again began to grow uncomfortable in the saddle. But she did not want to stop; she wanted to reach town while she knew she could still play her part with conviction. A two-day ride at least, if she was following the correct trail. Even of that she was not certain. She rode solely from memory.

Finally, though, her discomfort became so great that she had to pull her horse to a halt. It was starting to get dark and her seat and the inside legs of her pants felt worn plain through. She'd have to set up some sort of camp and spend the night alone. The thought filled her with trepidation. She had no weapon with which to defend herself—even if she knew how to fire a gun. She had her food and blankets and could probably build a sufficient fire, but those were just protection from hunger and the elements. She was completely helpless against any animal or human adversary. For the first time she grew angry at Walt for leaving her in this situation—isolated and unprotected.

She'd only been stopped for about an hour, shivering under the blankets not from the cold but from troubling emotions, when she heard the clopping of hoofbeats approaching across the dry flatlands.

Dawn tensed. The hoofbeats were getting nearer but she couldn't bring herself to turn her head in their direction. Her brain suddenly drained of all thought. All that she had so meticulously rehearsed emptied from her memory, like water pumped dry from a well.

Finally, she shifted her eyes and saw six riders coming toward her. The men slowed their horses and encircled her but did not dismount. Dawn didn't know who they were. She wasn't afraid as much as she was numb.

It was Deputy Blackie Collins who spoke first. "Are you Mrs. Harley? Dawn Harley?"

Dawn slowly pivoted her head toward him. She neither acknowledged with a word nor a gesture.

"Who else'd she be?" one of the riders said impatiently.

"Mrs. Harley, I'm Deputy Collins. From Colfax. I think you'd better be coming with us." His tone was hardly compassionate.

Dawn did not move. She couldn't. Her body felt strangely paralyzed. Collins finally climbed off his horse and walked over to her. He noticed how the girl was trembling, looked disheveled, and seemed to be almost in a state of shock.

When Collins next spoke a trace of sympathy filtered through in his words. "Mrs. Harley, we're here to take you back to town. We know what happened—to your husband."

Dawn flickered her eyes toward him.

"And we know who done it," Collins added. "One of 'em is a wanted criminal named Walt Egan." He paused, and then said cleverly: "But I think you know that, don't you, Mrs. Harley?"

Dawn's eyes widened and she attempted to speak, to say something in protest, but the words wouldn't come.

One of the posse got off his horse and walked over to a sack lying on the ground. He opened it, glanced inside, then looked up at Collins.

"Grub," he announced.

Collins turned to the woman. "Was that Egan's idea? To bring along food?" he asked.

The girl said nothing.

Collins was growing irritated by her reticence. "Or did you maybe offer?" he snapped.

"Ain't just grub," the man inspecting the sack suddenly snapped.

Collins turned to see the man withdraw a handful of bills from the sack.

" 'Bout a hundred dollars, looks like," the man said as he flipped his pudgy fingers through the currency. He examined one of the bills closely, then sniffed it. "Looks and smells like new issue. Like what that stage to Reno was carryin'."

Dawn swallowed, hard. Walt had obviously left her with a present of some of the money he and Sam Bond had stolen. *That* she knew she could not easily explain.

She refused to speak—or budge from her spot —and Collins finally had to help her to her feet. The girl did not resist.

"You wanta explain how you come by that money?" Collins asked her.

When she didn't reply, Collins said tightly: "No matter. You'll talk once we get you into town. Don't know what your part is in all this, but I aim to find out. That I can promise you."

He got her atop her horse and then turned his attention to two of his riders.

"Take Mrs. Harley back into Colfax," he instructed. "We're on the right trail and I wanta continue following it."

"What d'you want us to do with her?"

Collins' eyes narrowed and he looked hard at the girl. "There were three empty jail cells last time I looked."

Dawn returned eye contact but didn't speak.

"We can't go puttin' her in jail," one of the men

131

said in protest. "We don't know for sure that she done anythin'."

"She ain't cooperating," Collins returned bluntly.

"Well . . . maybe she can tell you what direction they went?" one of the posse suggested.

Collins gave the man a disapproving glance for suggesting how he should do his job, then he again looked at the girl.

"Givin' you another chance to speak up." His voice remained firm.

Dawn merely looked away.

"I wanta know which way they was goin' and if there are any others besides Egan," Collins demanded.

No answer.

Collins expelled a breath in frustration. He gave his head a shake. "Don't know if'n you can't talk—or you won't. But you ain't makin' this easy on yourself." He then spoke to his men: "We'll get answers outta her later." To the two riders he was sending back: "You'll be passin' the others on the way. Tell 'em we're on the trail and have 'em join up with us. Don't know how much of a lead Egan's got, but we've gotta get him 'fore he reaches the canyon."

CHAPTER SEVEN

Walt rode, and troubled thoughts traveled with him. What concerned him was the exact worry that had come upon Dawn: leaving her alone and without the means to protect herself. He tried to console himself with the belief that she'd make it back home with no difficulty—but he knew that he could not be sure. He also couldn't be certain that she wouldn't take it on herself to come riding after him.

But he couldn't allow himself to consider such thoughts. His main focus had to be on getting himself safely to Rooster Canyon and onward to Utah. Perhaps when the snows melted he would follow Dawn's plan and move northward. Not so far into Canada, but maybe up into the Dakotas. Maybe even give up his outlaw life and take a shot at respectability. He grinned unconsciously: That possibility seemed remote—almost beyond his comprehension. He simply knew no other way to live. In truth, he couldn't imagine finding any satisfaction in hanging up his guns.

Especially with Dawn not along to encourage him.

Once he got to the old codger's house in Utah he'd have all winter to decide his plans. No point in dwelling on the future yet. Besides, from his experience, the future was determined not by months, days . . . or even hours. But by minutes.

Just east of Rooster Canyon was the small town of Barron Creek. It was a pretty remote community with an over-the-hill lawman running things, and a place that once had the reputation as a safe stopover for outlaws, provided they didn't linger and could feed a few dollars into the community coffers—namely the sheriff's pocket. Walt decided to ride into town and stock up on a few supplies since he'd left everything back with Dawn.

He didn't require much food and could make the day's ride into Barron Creek without difficulty. He'd get a few items, maybe stop at the saloon for a beer, depending on how the town looked, and then quickly be on his way.

He sat on his mount behind a low, hilly ridge that overlooked Barron Creek and waited until dusk before he slowly rode into town.

It was a sleepy community and was particularly quiet at this hour. Walt was satisfied. The stores would soon be closing and most of the citizens were already at home for the night. He remembered that not much went on here; even the saloon business was slow. Travelers and outlaws provided most of the business. Walt paced his horse slowly down the main street and thought how Barron Creek was the perfect setting for a successful bank score. But to his knowledge the

Merchants and Consumer Bank had never been robbed because the take would be small and the risk certainly not worth it, particularly in light of the protection the town afforded men of Walt's breed. In fact, desperados were so aware of this that the bank could leave all of its deposits out on the street and chances were not a single dollar would be stolen.

Walt dismounted, hitched his horse to the railing outside of the Barron Creek General Store, and sauntered inside. The proprietor was just emptying the day's cash from the till in preparation of closing up. By habit Walt took a studied glance at the money as it was being counted out, noticing what a meager sum it appeared to be, and then went about his business, returning a pleasant "Howdy" to the proprietor's greeting. Walt purchased bread, cold meat, and jerky, and some candy that would provide quick energy and help quench his thirst. He paid for his items and quietly left the store. The proprietor never so much as looked twice at him. Walt felt comfortable enough to go down to the saloon and treat himself to that beer.

Not expecting any trouble and not choosing to call unwanted attention to himself, he left his gunbelt inside the saddlebag along with his food purchases. While only a short distance to the saloon, Walt climbed up on his horse and rode it over, tethering it to the post directly outside the swinging doors. He did this just as a precaution because Walt was never a man to take chances.

The saloon was dark and virtually empty. The place smelled of beer, tempting Walt's thirst even more, and had a relaxing ambience. He looked around. Just a few scattered patrons too absorbed in their conversation or drinking to give Walt more than a passing glance. Unlike many of the towns Walt had visited in his travels, Barron Creek was a place where everyone minded his own business. *Hell*, Walt thought, *Jesse James could have passed through here and no one would have noticed.*

He walked up to the counter, slapping his boot down on the floor railing, and asked for a beer and a shot of whiskey. The barkeep obliged and Walt deposited some silver on the counter's sticky surface. He then dropped another coin.

"Buy yourself a drink," Walt said. He was in a generous mood.

The barkeep looked at the coin, then up at Walt. "Thanks," he replied nonchalantly.

"Nice town," Walt commented idly.

The barkeep merely smiled and poured himself a shot of whiskey.

Walt exhaled a contented breath. "Yeah, nice . . . and quiet. Reckon you don't see much excitement here."

"No," the barkeep replied. "Like you say . . . it's pretty quiet."

Walt consumed both drinks swiftly. He decided to indulge himself to another beer. While waiting he rolled a cigarette. He felt relaxed and it was a feeling he could appreciate. In fact, he felt so at ease that he considered taking a room at the hotel and bedding down in comfort for the night. He was mighty tempted, but while Barron Creek might offer him protection, he didn't know who was on his trail. Or how far behind they were. One thing he *did* know was once a posse set out after him, if they were heading east, they would surely make a stopover in Barron Creek.

He kept focused on his drinking . . . until he heard a loud whoop of excitement emanate from off to his side. Walt turned his head in that direction and glanced into a little back room where he saw some men seated around a table playing cards. Next to robbing banks and stage-coaches, gambling was his passion—particularly poker. And while he couldn't allow himself the luxury of a night's stay at the hotel, he couldn't see the harm in playing a couple of hands with these locals. He was never averse to making some quick pocket cash. Walt finished his beer, tilted his hat up over his forehead, and walked into the room. He introduced himself as "Joe" and was instantly invited to join in.

The other players were quite intoxicated and within a half hour Walt had almost twenty-five dollars laid out before him on the table. One of the men was drunk and bitter enough to accuse the stranger of cheating. It was a common accusation leveled at Walt because of his extraordinary skill at cards. Still, Walt didn't want trouble. He merely fixed his accusor with a cold stare and soon the man appeared to back down.

"It's been my pleasure, gents," he said amiably. Then he got up from the table, gave each of the men a hard glance, and stepped from the room back into the saloon.

He'd just cleared the threshold when he heard the scrabble of chairs against the wood floor. He hardly had time to turn before he was tussled to the floor. All three of the card players had jumped him. Walt struggled against their hold and managed to break free. He scrambled to his feet and balanced himself, landing a hard punch against the jaw of one of the aggressors, sending him crashing back against the wall. But the other two men were on him quickly. Walt managed a knee to the groin at one of them, doubling the man over with a yelp of pain, but the third man slashed at him with both his fists, sending Walt reeling. He started to rise, but not fast enough. He only made it to his knees before all three were back on him, jerking him to his feet and slamming their fists into his face and belly. Walt tasted blood and within seconds his body grew limp under their relentless assault . . . and then a curtain of blackness descended over him. . . .

• • •

When he came to he was in a depressing cubicle he was not unfamiliar with. Three gray walls and a dim cast of light provided by a kerosene lantern through the opening of evenly spaced iron bars. He was stretched out on a plank that passed for a bunk and was suspended by chains hooked into either end of its length and fastened to the wall.

Walt seemed to hurt all over and it was with difficulty that he finally and stubbornly pulled himself into a sitting position. It seemed as if his whole body pulsed with pain. He worked his jaw and sat with his head hanging low, trying to pull his thoughts together, until he finally had the strength to raise his face and glance out into the adjoining room. It took him a few moments to regain his focus . . . and when he did, he didn't like what he saw.

The silhouette of a tall, lean man loomed before him, standing just several feet beyond the bars.

"Sorry 'bout the cramped accommodations," he said, "but we ain't had much reason to extend our hospitality lately. In fact, you're the first 'guest' we've had in quite a while."

Walt just lowered his head again and gave it a shake. He wasn't much in the mood to appreciate this fellow's brand of humor.

"You can count yourself lucky you weren't heeled, otherwise chances are you'd be in a box a whole lot tighter than this," the man said as he walked closer toward the cell, revealing himself more fully.

He was wearing a sheriff's badge.

Walt felt a tightness grip his gut. As the cloudiness cleared from his eyes he noticed that this man was not the Barron Creek lawman he remembered.

"You're . . . makin' some kinda mistake, mister," Walt said, speaking around the shooting pain in his jaw. "I—I was just passin' through and stopped in for a—"

The man interrupted. "First off, friend, let's get it straight out who you're talkin' to. I ain't no 'mister.' The name's Percy. Sheriff Sebastian Percy."

Walt drew and exhaled a defeated breath.

"And it's *you* what made the mistake," the sheriff added. "Yeh, by tryin' to cheat the Allison brothers at cards. They ain't the brightest stars in the sky, but they're kin and they stick together"— he tightly clamped the fingers of both hands together for emphasis—"like this. Hadda you been wearin' a gun they wouldn'ta bothered trying to take you in a fair fight like they done. They'da shot you dead on the spot. Maybe bad for them, but a whole lot worse for you." He grinned, exposing a mouthful of gapped teeth.

"I—don't call bein' jumped by three men a fair fight," Walt said miserably, scraping crusts of blood from the edge of his mouth.

"That ain't of no matter," the sheriff said dismissively. "But you bein' here is."

"Yeah?"

The sheriff straightened his posture, stiffly, as if he had a sore back.

"Make it my business to do a check on strangers —'specially troublemakers," he explained. "Make it my prime responsibility, in fact, given the way this town used to be run. Keep abreast of all the bulletins that reach my office too, unlike my late predecessor. Noticed that saddlebag of yours hangin' a little low. Took a look see and I reckon you can guess what I found inside." The sheriff's face went rigid. "Can't you, *Egan?*"

Walt knew he was caught but still attempted a play at ignorance. "Egan? You're speakin' to the wrong man, Sheriff. Name's—Paul. Charlie Paul."

But Sheriff Percy was a smart and perceptive lawman and wasn't buying any of his lying protests. "Second mistake you made was stayin' in town just a little too long."

And Walt conceded with regret that he had. The sheriff had him dead to rights and there wasn't a thing he could do.

Except wait for the posse to show up.

CHAPTER EIGHT

Many miles away in Colfax, Dawn was placed inside her own jail cell, and a cell only a tad more comfortable than the one Walt was occupying in Barron Creek. She'd been "escorted" back into town briskly, with no stop for rest, and all during the ride the only sensation of which she had been aware was the aching soreness of her butt and the scalding along the tender skin of her thighs. The pain was almost more than she could endure but she refused to complain. She could barely walk once she managed to maneuver herself off the horse outside the marshal's office. Her obvious discomfort was noticed by one of the men who had rode in with her and he took sympathy on her, sending for Doc Speer, who came over to the jail and prescribed a lotion treatment that she was allowed to smooth on in privacy. Doc Speer also insisted to the jailer that a soft down pillow be given to her so that she would not have to sit herself on the hardness of the bunk.

Later that afternoon Dawn received a visit from Judge Reynolds, who tried in as kindly a way as possible to question her. He was a stern man, befitting his profession, but both his face and his voice were gentle as he talked to her. His sympathy for the loss of her husband seemed genuine and she felt he would be compassionate to her case, but she was still too numb from her ordeal to provide him with what he wanted to know. Mostly, she remained hurt and confused over Walt's desertion . . . and worried over his safety. She feared that if the posse caught up with him, they'd never give him a fair chance.

After Reynolds was through, he spoke quietly to Hoss Lambert, the man who was given the responsibility of watching the jail in Blackie Collins' absence.

"There's no reason for this girl to be in a jail cell," he admonished him.

Hoss scratched his head and spoke slowly and with ignorance. "I kinda feel that way too, Judge. But those were the instructions we got from Blackie . . . uh, Deputy Collins."

Reynolds shifted his eyes toward the girl standing in the cell with her back to the bars, and he shook his head. "I want her released into my care," he ordered. "We don't know all the facts and I can guarantee you we won't find out anything with her locked up in there. Open the door."

"So—what you're sayin' is that you'll be the one takin' responsibili—" Hoss was loyal and trustworthy, but somewhat slow-witted.

"Yes, that's what I'm saying, you idiot," Reynolds snapped impatiently.

While Hoss went to get the keys, Judge Reynolds stepped back over to the bars of the cell. "Until we get this all sorted out, Mrs. Harley, you'll be coming home with me."

Dawn stayed with the judge and his wife at their modest wood-framed house just on the outskirts of town. It was a house that very much reminded Dawn of the home she had shared with Jed. Quaint and unpretentious but neat and comfortable.

During that time Jed was laid to rest in a hilltop cemetery. Most of the town, folks who had liked and respected Jed Harley, came to pay their final respects. Dawn did not attend. Her absence was noted by the people of Colfax, which only generated more suspicion among them about her involvement in his murder, based on the dying words of her husband. The judge tried to pacify the community by publicly explaining that Mrs. Harley still remained too traumatized to appear at the burial.

Judge Reynolds hoped that his kindness and particularly the gentle, caring nature of his wife might break through to the girl so that she would reveal what she knew. But while Dawn gradually began to emerge from what was perceived as her protective shell, she steadfastly claimed not to have any recollection of what had happened from the day her husband was killed. In fact, it appeared that she possessed no memory of Jed Harley ever having been murdered.

It was merely a facade. A convenient way for her to avoid those questions she was not willing to answer.

Of course there were some who questioned the validity of her condition. Her forgetfulness seemed a little too convenient. But Dawn continued to feign her 'amnesia'—until the day the whooping posse rode back into Colfax bringing along a manacled Walt Egan as their prisoner.

People rapidly congregated on the main street, employees and customers emerging from the various stores and businesses to see what all the excitement was about. Within minutes the scene took on almost a circuslike atmosphere. There was cheering for the posse . . . and jeering at the outlaw.

The posse had indeed stopped over in Barron Creek and, much to their surprise, found their quarry, severely beaten from the saloon fight, confined to a jail cell. The sheriff had explained the circumstances surrounding Walt's arrest and Deputy Collins explained why they were hunting the outlaw. Both Egan and the money from the stagecoach holdup were turned over to the posse and the men rode back to Colfax in victory.

Walt was swiftly hustled into a jail cell by Blackie Collins, who then proudly went out into the street to receive the congratulations of the townsfolk. He enjoyed the new respect given him by the citizens and naturally did not hasten to reveal that the real work had been done by the quick thinking sheriff of Barron Creek. He likewise had advised the men in his posse not to tarnish their moment of glory by letting on the truth. Of course he knew that Walt himself may at some point say something—but that didn't worry him. Who would take seriously the word of a thief and a murderer?

Leaving extra men to guard the jail, Collins immediately rode out to see Judge Reynolds. He was startled when the butler admitted him into the house and he saw Dawn Harley having tea in the sun-bright front parlor with both the judge and his wife.

Dawn's complexion went pale as her sad, doe-like eyes fell upon the deputy. Her body suddenly became weak and she dropped the ornate teacup to the floor, shattering it. She tried to brace her-self for the news she did not want to hear.

The judge noticed Dawn's reaction and, leaving his wife to tend to her, ushered Collins into the kitchen, where they could talk out of earshot.

Before Collins could announce his capture of Walt Egan, the judge took the opportunity to berate him.

"I understand it was you who ordered Mrs. Harley put into a cell."

"We located her on the trail . . . and she wouldn't cooperate," Collins explained simply, if uncomfortably.

"How do you know the criminals didn't just leave her there, having no more use for her as a hostage?" the judged questioned. "Surely you must have seen the condition she was in."

Collins nodded. He felt properly chastised. Somewhat humiliated, though he tried not to let it upset him.

"Well . . . yeh, but we knew she'd been with Egan, and maybe closer than we figgered, given that we found some of that stagecoach money in her possession—though she wouldn't tell us nothin'. There wasn't time to pry any answers outta her 'cause we hadda get back on his trail. I thought maybe puttin' her in a cell might scare her enough to get her to talkin'."

Judge Reynolds gave the deputy a look of disapproval. "Well, you handled *that* wrong, Collins. Whatever went on that day her husband and Sheriff Thornton were killed, and whatever happened afterward, we won't be judging her 'til all the facts come out." The judge paused and gave Collins a penetrating stare. "Which I hope you've brought me."

Collins relaxed and nodded. "Better'n that. We brought in Egan."

Judge Reynolds' stern expression instantly dissipated. Now he looked pleased.

"Alive?"

"Yessir. Recovered that stage money too."

"Any others besides Egan?"

"Looks like he was the only one," Collins answered. "Though he ain't talkin' much, either."

"Well, there really isn't much he *needs* to be telling us," the judge said. "Except if Mrs. Harley had any part in this."

When Judge Reynolds stepped back into the parlor and informed his wife and Dawn of Walt Egan's capture, he observed the girl closely, hoping to gauge a reaction.

Dawn tried to maintain an impassive expression that would betray nothing more than a flicker of surprise at hearing of his arrest, but the judge's discerning eye also noticed a heavy bob of her Adam's apple as she forced down a swallow. It was a telling gesture, though not identifying precisely what emotion she was feeling. The doubt still lingered within the judge. Was it relief . . . or perhaps despair at his capture?

Reynolds decided on another, less subtle, way to get at the truth. He told Dawn that he would be going to the marshal's office within the hour and needed her to come with him to identify Walt Egan as the man who had taken her hostage and who perhaps was also responsible for the murders of her husband and the sheriff. Dawn tentatively agreed, understanding that if she refused it would only create further suspicion. But even her momentary reluctance set the judge's brain to thinking. She didn't appear fearful at the prospect of seeing Egan—a reaction he could have understood and accepted. Instead, her hesitation seemed to suggest something more. Something . . . almost personal between them. Possibly the clue to what Jed Harley had meant with his dying words.

During the wait Dawn struggled to keep her

composure. She wasn't afraid for herself. She knew that Walt would protect her. But even that wasn't important to her. What worried Dawn was that she couldn't trust her own emotions. To see Walt behind bars, facing a fate that he himself had acknowleged was already sealed, a fate he confessed dreading more than dying under gunfire . . . would prove to much for her to bear. She knew that what she might expose upon seeing him would be all the evidence the town would need to find her as guilty as Walt. And again, that didn't matter. But Walt hadn't wanted that for her. She remembered how he'd said that he couldn't die with that on his conscience. She had to find it in herself to be strong—for him.

It instantly all became clear to her. Why he had left her on the trail. He hadn't deserted her; rather, he'd chosen to spare her his misery. He must have known that his days were numbered and did not want her to be a part of that final outcome. It was never selfishness or uncaring. Sitting in solitude inside the comfortable parlor of the judge's house Dawn now recognized that his motive had only been consideration for her. That he did care for her. And coming to this realization Dawn could now admit wholeheartedly that she loved Walt.

And she did not want to see him die.

He had spared her. Now she had to find a way to save him . . . from the hangman's noose.

CHAPTER NINE

Dawn knew what she was going to do. What she must do. As difficult as it would be for her she was going to follow through with Walt's request and "betray" him. She would say that Walt Egan had taken her as a hostage. It wouldn't really matter . . . because as she and Judge Reynolds rode in the buggy toward the jailhouse she had already formulated her plan.

She walked close beside the judge, through the curious crowd congregated outside, many of whom regarded her with cold, accusing stares, and went inside the brick faced building. Deputy Collins and several men were there and Dawn avoided looking at Collins. She also took her time raising her eyes to the cell that held Walt. When she finally did, she saw him seated on his bunk. He looked at her, his expression merely a grim mask, revealing no more than a dull, morose look. His face was a battered mess and Dawn had to suppress a gasp. She assumed that he had been beaten by the posse. He looked as helpless as she had ever seen a man, and it both saddened and angered her.

Finally Walt stood up, and he edged over to the bars.

"Hello, Mrs. Harley," he said. His voice was

flat, as emotionless as the expression he maintained.

Dawn said nothing, though she could feel the judge's eyes steady on her.

"Is this the man?" Judge Reynolds asked.

Before Dawn could bring herself to answer, Walt spoke up.

"Why ask her? I admit it. Killed her husband and took her with me."

Dawn's doe like eyes flashed with surprise. She opened her mouth to speak—to protest his claim that it was he who had killed Jed, but once again Walt's words intercepted hers.

"And just to clear things up, it was also me that killed your sheriff."

Judge Reynolds turned his eyes from Walt and looked firmly at Dawn. "I want to hear it from you, Mrs. Harley," he said. "Is what Egan's saying true?"

Dawn hesitated.

"Go ahead and tell 'em, Mrs. Harley," Walt said smoothly. "You *know* it ain't gonna make no difference now."

Dawn understood what Walt was saying. No one else in the room could know, but Walt's words—his simple yet effective prefacing of "You *know*" held a meaning for her.

She braced herself and locked her eyes deeply into Walt's, hoping to likewise speak to him through their expression.

And she knew that she succeeded. While to the men assembled Walt's face betrayed nothing more than resignation, Dawn herself could see in just the faintest, familiar way that he understood and appreciated her private message to him.

And finally she could say to the judge: "Yes, it's true."

The left corner of Walt's mouth curved upward in a slanted smile that said to her: "You did good." Then he turned and walked back over to his bunk.

The judge shifted his eyes from Dawn to Deputy Collins. They exchanged a look, but neither spoke.

Later that day the judge and the deputy met privately at a corner table at the saloon. Collins drank a mug of beer while Judge Reynolds spooned sugar into a cup of hot tea, garnished with a wedge of lemon. Collins was munching rather messily on a pickled egg as he talked. The judge, who had a delicate stomach, kept his focus away from his companion as Collins chewed aggressively on his lunch.

"I still ain't satisfied," Collins said through a mouthful of egg. "I think Egan's protectin' that girl."

The judge sipped on his tea with a thoughtful expression.

"Jed Harley didn't say what he said for no reason," Collins added with a blunt jab of his finger.

"No—he wouldn't say that without a reason," the judge agreed. "But I'm not convinced that girl's a murderer."

"So then how do *you* figger it?" Collins asked, wiping the beer from his mouth with a sweeping gesture of his hand.

"Jealousy maybe. A resentment spoken with Jed's dying breath. I'll concede there's likely an attraction between Egan and Dawn Harley. And I'll also say this much: I believe that she went along willingly with Egan." Judge Reynolds paused, took a breath. "But I've gotten to know that girl a bit, and I've got a hunch that if she was in any way involved she's going to eventually come clean."

Collins thumped his beer mug down hard on the table, turning the heads of a few of the other patrons in his direction. "Well, I think we should just come out and tell her what Jed said. See how she answers that."

Reynolds gave his head a shake. "No, Collins, that'd be wrong at this point. It'd be like we're outright accusing her."

"Which is what we should be doin', instead of all this pussyfootin'," Collins said in frustration.

"I want this straightened out as badly as you do," the judge assured him. "But we can't be accusing her of something she may be innocent of."

"Innocent?" Collins said, barely concealing his disgust. He swallowed the rest of his beer, set

153

the mug on the table, and took a probing look at the judge. "I'm startin' to think you really believe she is," he remarked.

"I'm not sure," the judge said, sighing. "But I do want to handle this fairly. Give her the benefit of the doubt."

"Well . . . just don't be forgettin', Judge, no one went 'fair' on either Jed Harley or Sheriff Thornton," Collins said piercingly.

Judge Reynolds' eyes momentarily flashed hard as his gaze fixed on the deputy. Then their intensity softened. He eased back in his chair, slowly rocked his head, and said in a pensive tone: "I know."

Collins asked: "So what're you gonna do 'til she decides to come clean? That is, *if* she ever does fess up."

Judge Reynolds took a few moments to consider his answer.

"Send her home, if she's ready."

Collins looked incredulous. "Send her home!"

The judge nodded. "That's right. Back to the farm. She'll be all alone out there. Alone with her conscience."

Alone with her conscience.

Alone maybe. But her conscience wasn't troubling her. At least not where Jed was concerned. The guilt she felt for her part in his death had been buried before her husband was.

154

Her concern now was for Walt. His trial had been swiftly set owing to the public's demand for justice, and she had to work fast.

Returning to the farm she didn't experience any feelings of unease at the violence that had occurred there. Four dead men . . . *murdered* men had lain inside her house. At one time she would never have gone back. But she had changed. She was not the girl she had been only a few short weeks ago. Strangely, it was as if she couldn't even recognize that person anymore. Someone naive, living in denial. Now she was stronger, determined, and remained of a singular purpose. Her focus was fixed only on what she must do.

When she entered the house the first thing she did was break open the locked drawer of the bureau and remove Jed's preloaded Navy Colt revolver. She also discovered an unopened box of .36 caliber round lead balls and other para-phernalia she did not understand next to the gun. Luckily, after searching a little further, she came upon a user's manual. Dawn had never held a gun in her life, much less fired one, but in the days that followed she set about learning the intricacies of loading the single-action weapon and practicing its discharge with a firm determi-nation. Even though her house was miles away from any neighbors who might hear the gunfire, she still rode out far into the country to a secluded spot where she could begin honing her skill.

First, she had to grow comfortable with the feel of a handgun. Then steady herself against the sharp report as she fingered and pulled the trigger. It wasn't important that she become proficient at using it—just that she appear confident enough holding a gun to convince Deputy Collins and whoever else might be at the jailhouse when she rode up of her intention.

She attended Walt's trial only once—when she was again asked to identify Walt Egan before the court and also to provide a brief testimony. She made the identification but once more claimed a memory loss as to what had happened at the house. She couldn't remember who had killed her husband. Of course her apparent "forgetfulness" would have no bearing on the outcome. The trial itself was merely a formality. Walt especially knew it, and he looked pleased that Dawn had not incriminated herself.

She wasn't present on the day of sentencing—when Judge Reynolds, bedecked in a black robe, the stern demeanor he had worn throughout the trial now heightened, solemnly condemned Walt Egan to death by hanging. The hanging would occur in town—a public execution. The packed courtroom erupted in wild cheers as the judge passed down the sentence and the manner in which it would be rendered. The ruckus was such that Judge Reynolds had to bang the gavel several times to restore order to the proceedings. Deputy

Blackie Collins heaved a sigh of relief. It had been his concern that if the trial had not reached this outcome—and soon—he might have to contend with a lynch mob.

There was great celebration in Colfax. Workers hastily went to work constructing the gallows outside the courthouse. Folks came from throughout the territory to witness the hanging of the last member of the infamous Chancer Gang, whose exploits had both terrorized and intrigued the Southwest. Hotels, saloons, and restaurants enjoyed a brisk business.

Walt spent most of the two days preceding his execution restlessly pacing his cell. His deep-rooted terror at "strangling at the end of a rope" intensified as the hours slowly ticked by. From the barred window embedded high in the north side wall of his cell he could hear the relentless building of the scaffold and the sounds of people urging the workmen to work faster. The construction seemed to go on around the clock, and with the incessant banging and hammering coupled with the festivities that went on all night at the saloon and even out in the streets it was impossible for Walt to get any sleep—if there were any way that he could. But he was unable to relax enough to grab even ten minutes of shut-eye. To try and get his mind off of what was ahead, he focused much of his thinking on Dawn. The kind of girl she was. Despite her genteel appearance and nature, she was truly a gal full of guts and grit. He admired how she was willing to stick it out with him. No woman he had ever known would have been of a mind to ride with him and take the chances that she had been prepared to take. He savored the memory of those two nights they had camped out together, just the two of them—and now regretted his decision to leave her. Things probably would have been a whole lot different. He never would have had to ride into Barron Creek for supplies —and if he had, never would have stopped in at the saloon and given in to the temptation of a game of poker. He'd made a lot of bad decisions in his life, but abandoning Dawn that night was surely the worst choice he'd ever made.

He became momentarily melancholy. He breathed out deeply. He only hoped she would find herself a good life.

Walt was determined not to expose the fear he was feeling in front of the jailers, who guarded him in four-hour rotation shifts. He was occasionally taunted, and reminded—often graphically—of what was to come, but he maintained an outward bravado. He would not give them the satisfaction of branding him a coward.

Late on the afternoon the day before the hanging, Walt was paid a visit by Blackie Collins. Collins had not been around much, leaving the care of the prisoner to the trusted men who had rode in the posse, while he himself was celebrated at various town events. With the Chancer Gang all dead, Collins had no worry about any renegade trying to break Walt out of jail.

Today it was just Collins and Walt. He'd sent the jailers home since he wanted to be alone with the prisoner in his final hours. It was not only his duty . . . it was his pleasure. He'd brought over a hot meal from the restaurant for Walt, who refused even to consider it. His refusal, however, did not prevent Collins from enjoying his own dinner of a bowl of chili and steamed biscuits. And after a long silence, the deputy finally got up from the marshal's desk that he'd been promised he would soon be occupying, and walked over to the cell, holding his bowl of chili. All of a sudden he was grinning like a Cheshire cat. Walt sat on his bunk and regarded him peculiarly, with squinting eyes.

Collins said: "Y'know Egan, when I saw you sittin' in that jail in Barron's Creek, I confess I wanted to walk right over and shake your hand."

Walt's dark eyes narrowed deeper, almost into slits. He had no idea what the deputy was talking about. Neither was he particularly curious.

"That's a fact," Collins added expansively. "You don't know it, but I owe you a lot. It's all on account of you I'm gonna be appointed the new marshal of our fair community." With his fingers wide he smoothed the palm of his hand along the left side of his chest. "Yeh, and that tin star'll fit me just fine."

Walt looked at him with an expression of disdain.

Collins sighed. "Kinda sad when you think 'bout it. All this excitement goin' on 'cause of you . . . yet in a week, maybe less, you'll be forgotten. Well . . . if it's any consolation, I won't be forgettin'."

"No consolation," Walt said dryly.

"Reckon not." Collins spooned up some of his chili, which he slurped into his mouth, and took a few steps closer to the bars. He lowered his voice. "But tell me, Egan. Now that you ain't got nothin' to lose . . . just what went on 'tween you and that Harley girl?"

Walt's eyes snapped angrily toward the deputy.

Collins' gaze shifted around the office, merely for effect since no one else was present, and he spoke in a conspiratorial tone. "I'll tell you what: You fess up and I give you my word no one will ever know what you told me."

"Just be our little secret, huh?" Walt smirked.

"Give you my word," Collins said, the transparent sincerity fairly dripping off his words.

Walt leaned back on his bunk, against the wall with his knees pulled up, and looked straight ahead at the gray wall with a grim smile pasted on his face. "Your word ain't worth spit," he said. "Anyway, gonna have to disappoint you, *Deputy*,

160

but Mrs. Harley and me already told the court what 'went on,' as you put it."

Collins smiled back. "Neat little story too. But I can tell you . . . ain't too many believe it."

"Nothin' I can do 'bout that," Walt shrugged.

Collins nodded. "Well, 'course we could also play this another way."

Walt's eyes slowly veered in his direction. He didn't like the sneaky tone that had crept into Collins' voice.

The deputy explained. "If you're not of a mind to tell me, I could, in my new position as city marshal, make life . . . well, let's say somewhat unpleasant for the lady."

Walt made himself look unaffected by the threat, though inside he was seething, his guts all coiled up like a snake getting ready to strike.

But he merely said: "Ain't no concern of mine."

"You sure 'bout that?" Collins returned deviously.

Walt spoke slowly. "I killed her husband—and your marshal—and took the girl along with me as a cover 'til it was safe. There ain't no more to it."

"No feelin's for her, eh?"

Walt returned his focus to the granite wall of his cell.

Collins twisted his neck to look at the ticking wall clock in the office. He drew a deep breath that inflated his chest. "Not much time left," he remarked. "But I'll be here all night, in case you should change your mind."

Walt ignored what he was saying and instead asked: "Y'gotta smoke?"

Collins shook his head. "No."

"But you could get me one?"

"Could," Collins said with a smug smile.

Walt watched the deputy turn and walk back to his desk, and he spit contemptuously on the floor.

Dusk came early, followed by the autumn night. There were heavy clouds rolling across the sky that Walt could just glimpse from the barred window of his cell. He grew reflective, remembering how he used to enjoy camping out under such clouds. Particularly after a successful bank job when he and his partners would find themselves a secluded little spot and celebrate all night. Now they all were dead . . . and he was next. The one who feared hanging the most of the bunch and, ironically, the only one now set to die that way. He suffered the further realization that the next time he saw daylight would be his last. Again he descended into melancholy. So much that he had taken for granted he was now going to miss about this world.

The streets seemed quiet and an uncommon stillness hung over the town after all the preceding nights of festivity. Walt figured that everyone was resting up for the early morning hanging. Then they'd enjoy another celebration . . . and then

Collins was probably right: He'd be quickly forgotten.

Maybe even by Dawn.

He got up from the bunk and started to pace. As his melancholy passed, his nerves once again started to get the better of him. Alone, the courage he'd exhibited in front of Collins and the others was swiftly deserting him. He had begun to perspire even though the night air that drifted in through the bars of the overhead window was cool. He wanted to call out to Deputy Collins for the time, then quickly decided it was probably better he didn't know. Quiet . . . so quiet that Walt could hear the rapid thumping of his heart in his chest. There seemed to be no way he could steady his heartbeat—or calm himself. His thoughts traced back to Barron Creek and the mistake he'd made not carrying his gun into the saloon. He could have outdrawn those yokels, and even if they or the sheriff had got him, at least it would have been over quickly. He could accept dying by a gun, but the image of the hanging he'd seen in Tombstone had never left him. He prided himself as a man without fear, yet the memory of that poor soul helplessly fighting against the choking of the rope continued to haunt his nightmares.

And within just hours that same fate would befall him. . . .

A short time later Collins got up from his desk,

yawned and stretched, and stepped over to the cell while Walt was still pacing.

"Scared yet, Egan?" he asked with a cruel inflection.

Walt didn't answer, tried to ignore him. But it seemed that Collins was bored and seeking some entertainment by attempting to provoke him.

"Yeh, you're scared," he said with a subtle cock of his head. "Can see it on you. Can even smell it. Can't say I blame you, though. Don't know what it'd be like to sit out your kind of wait." He craned his neck for a look at the time. "Almost eleven. That makes—what? Another seven hours?"

Walt spun around to him with a stone-edged expression.

Collins smiled. "Bet you'd like a drink, huh? Somethin' to calm your nerves. Actually I could use a belt myself right about now. Whaddaya say?"

And suddenly—instinctively—fueled by an overwhelming rage toward the taunting lawman, Walt lunged at the bars, gripping so tightly at the rusty iron that the fingers of both hands reddened. He skewered Collins with an expression frightening in its intensity. Collins could see his fury and knew without a doubt that he'd try to kill him with his bare hands if he got the chance. But he was protected by the bars and calmly took a step backward.

Still, this aggressive move against him gave Collins another opportunity to further twist Walt's screws.

"Know why I'm gonna make a good marshal, Egan?" he said coldly, hissing the words through his teeth. "'Cause I hate outlaw scum. Shoulda put a bullet in you back on the trail. Yeh, coulda done that and said you was tryin' to make a break. That'd be just cause. But that also woulda been too easy. I like it better this way . . . and the same'll go for all your type that rides into Colfax."

There was a gentle knocking at the door. Collins frowned, looked momentarily puzzled.

"Now who do you figure that could be?" he said with dramatic emphasis.

He smirked at Walt and went over to answer the knock, saying as he walked: "Can guarantee you one thing, Egan. It ain't no reprieve."

With a hand poised against the six-shooter in his holster, Collins unlocked the door and slowly opened it a crack.

It was Dawn Harley. She was wearing her battered brown Stetson and was dressed in a buckskin jacket and loose-fitting work pants.

"I'd . . . like to see Walt Egan," she said politely.

Collins chuckled. "I bet you would."

But he also looked doubtful. He remained suspect of Dawn Harley and didn't trust her. He kept the girl standing outside for several moments until he gave his head a determined shake and said: "Sorry, Mrs. Harley. The condemned ain't allowed no visitors. 'Cept the parson." He glanced over his shoulder at Walt. "But he don't wanta see him." He started to shut the door.

"No, wait," Dawn said firmly, pressing the palm of her hand against the outside of the door. "It's important." She drew in a deep breath. "He's gotta tell you the truth about what happened. He can't be hanged before telling you—"

She suddenly looked unsteady on her feet, like she was about to pass out. And at that Collins swung open the door to catch her. She crumpled like a rag doll into his arms, moaning, her left hand tightly gripping the handbag she carried with what appeared her last ounces of strength. Collins dragged her inside. He seated her on the chair behind his desk then turned to fetch a glass of water from the pitcher on the far counter.

It was all the time Dawn needed. By the time Collins turned back to her with the water she had reached inside her handbag and withdrawn the Navy Colt revolver. She thumbed the hammer back to full cock and aimed it at the deputy with an expression that was icy cold. Her eyes were hard and her lips drawn tight.

"Drop that gunbelt you're wearing and open the cell," she commanded.

Collins stood looking at her, dumbfounded.

Walt's relief was such that he could not contain his amusement. "Standin' there with your jaw hangin' open while a girl—uh, pardon, Dawn—a *woman* holds a gun on you," he said jubilantly. "Yeh, you'll make a crackerjack marshal, Collins."

"I'm willing to shoot you dead on the spot unless you do as I say," Dawn warned the deputy.

"I'd be advisin' you to do *just* as she says," Egan said. "'Cause she just made herself one of 'us,' Collins. And that means she ain't got nothin' to lose."

Although her insides were trembling like jelly and her nerves were taut, Dawn looked completely composed. For just a fraction of a second Collins considered calling her bluff and drawing on her. But he studied her carefully and believed she could—and *would* make good on her threat. He had no choice but to comply. He unfastened his gunbelt and let it drop to the floor. Dawn instructed him to kick it far aside, and he did. She then got up from the chair, stepped over to the side of the desk, and tossed him the big ring that held the keys to the cells.

Collins slowly walked over to the cage that held Walt. He was terrified. Terrified of what Walt would do to him once he was freed. He'd seen the true look of a killer when Walt had jumped at him earlier. He couldn't even raise his eyes to Walt, just kept looking at his fingers while he

167

fumbled for the right key. But he could hear Walt's heavy breathing, which sounded like a predatory beast getting ready to pounce once released.

Walt read into his apprehension. "I oughta put a bullet in you, Collins," he said through gritted teeth. "Wouldn't make a bit of difference to my case." He let the deputy sweat for a few extra moments, then he said: "But I ain't gonna hurt you. Just gotta keep you quiet 'til sunup."

Collins' mouth was dry. "You'll never make it, Egan. You won't get far 'fore the whole territory's after you."

"Mebbe. But if'n that happens at least I'll be choosin' the way I wanta go. And I promise you it won't be at the end of no rope."

With his eyes still lowered, Collins fit the key into the lock. It took a couple of tries since his hand was not steady.

He hesitated. "And you know they won't go easy on the lady."

Walt glanced over at Dawn, who looked at him reassuringly.

Walt's own expression went grim. "The lady made her choice."

Once Collins got the door to the cell open he started to step aside. But Walt moved forward in a flash, grabbing the deputy's wrist with his left hand and tugging him inside. He clenched his right hand into a fist and plowed it dead center into Collins' gut. The deputy howled and doubled over. Walt pulled him upright and then delivered a solid punch to the side of his head. It connected with a cracking sound. All of the hatred he felt toward the deputy for his torment and the threat against Dawn went into the blow and Collins' neck snapped back as his eyes rolled up in their sockets, and he started to crumple. For good measure, Walt thrust him upward by the collar once more and belted him again. Already unconscious from the force of the first blow, Collins dropped limply to the floor like a sack of flour when Walt released him. Walt dragged him over to the bunk.

"Get the cuffs outta the drawer," he instructed Dawn.

Walt manacled Collins' hands behind his back and tied the deputy's own kerchief tightly around his mouth, as a gag. He glanced over his shoulder at Dawn.

"Reckon I don't need to ask if you got any of that money I left you with?" he said.

Dawn gave her head a slow shake.

Walt reached into both of Collins' pants pockets and finally pulled out the few dollars he had on his person. Then he locked him inside the cell and pocketed the keys.

"Should buy us a few hours," Walt said to the girl as he lifted the deputy's gunbelt from the floor and strapped it on. He pulled out the revolver and flipped open the cylinder, checking for bullets. The gun was loaded. He snapped it closed and thrust it into the holster. "But we gotta ride like the wind. I'll have to take Collins' horse 'til I can trade off later."

Dawn was silent the whole time Walt took care of his preparations. He removed an extra box of .44 shells and another box of rifle cartridges from the desk, then grabbed a Winchester from the gun rack. Finally he retrieved his Stetson from the hat rack and his black leather riding gloves from one of the drawers. He slid the gloves over his fingers smoothly, with a precision that Dawn found somewhat fascinating. Just as she found *everything* about Walt Egan intriguing.

One last detail. He grabbed the deputy's duster from the wall peg on which it was hanging. The only clothes he had were what he was wearing: his pants, shirt, and brown leather vest. He and Collins were about the same size and the duster should fit him fine and keep him warm against the night. When he was ready to leave, he stopped long enough to gaze at the girl. He nodded and smiled his thanks, then swept her into his arms for a quick embrace.

He said: "You know, Dawn, it's true what I said. Now for sure there won't be no turnin' back. I just hope you won't regret what you done."

Dawn spoke surely. "I knew what I was doing. I won't be having any regrets."

And then she gave in to the desire that had

been flooding through her and she pressed her lips full against his.

Walt allowed for only a brief kiss before he gently pulled her back with a smile. "There'll be plenty of time for that later," he said.

He did a quick yet thorough study of her eyes. There was no doubt. No apprehension. Just the sincere determination he expected, which confirmed to Walt that she would stay beside him until whatever proved their eventual destiny.

"Okay," Walt said gently. "Better take a gander outside."

Dawn opened the door to the office and peered out onto the main street, scanning both directions. The street looked deserted, though about a block away she could just make out the shadowy forms of some people standing outside the saloon. They were loud and seemed too inebriated to notice them.

She and Walt stepped outdoors carefully. Walt gave her a lift onto her mount and then rammed the Winchester into the scabbard fastened to the saddle of Collins' mare. He unlooped the reins from the hitching rail and climbed up. They rode quietly down the street, keeping the pace of their horses slowed to an easy trot so as not to call attention to themselves—until, at last, they reached the eastern edge of town where they spurred their horses into a gallop.

CHAPTER TEN

Blackie Collins remained unconscious until almost sunup. And when he finally revived, his face felt as if it had been pummeled by a battering ram. In his first clear moment of consciousness he was sure that his jaw had been broken. He carefully tried to work the muscles under the tightness of the kerchief, and although it hurt like hell, he couldn't be certain whether his jawbone was still intact.

In the next instant he recalled through a blurry haze what had happened, and considered the consequences—to himself and to his career.

He quickly became numb to any physical pain.

They'd be arriving soon: the judge, members of the council, the volunteers . . . and they'd find *him* inside the cell that Walt Egan had been occupying. Handcuffed and helpless. He'd have to tell them the truth, but they wouldn't look favorably on a lawman hoping for the marshal's job who allowed himself to be tricked and humiliated by a woman.

He thought miserably that he could surely forget about the appointment. He'd be lucky if he was permitted to stay on as deputy. But if that was how it had to be, he would accept it. As long as he could join in the hunt for Walt Egan . . . and

Dawn Harley. That much he believed was owed him. He now had a personal score to settle.

And this time, the minute he got the chance, he'd make sure neither of them would be riding back to a jail cell.

Come daybreak Walt and Dawn were many miles from Colfax. They were heading southeast, toward hill country, though uncertain of their destination. But they had no choice but to keep riding. They couldn't chance even an hour's rest until it got dark. Fortunately, Dawn had brought along water, feed for the horses, and sufficient supplies.

After racing their horses in a gallop for the better part of their ride to give themselves a strong distance from their pursuers, they finally slowed their mounts and had rode for the last several miles at an easier pace. The horses had their heads half-lowered and their hoofbeats were muffled in the dry sand.

The cool, fresh morning air and the pristine purity of the open desert country that stretched before them relaxed the pair. Walt especially savored the freedom of his surroundings. For a man just hours from being hanged, he was feeling pretty good.

At one point later in their journey, Walt, eyes ahead, said to the girl: "You know the first thing I think we oughta be doin'?"

Dawn looked at him, curious.

"Find a preacher and get ourselves married," he suggested matter-of-factly.

Dawn was flabbergasted. When she could finally speak, she said: "Now's not the time to be thinking of *that*."

Walt replied quickly: "I ain't meanin' now. I'm talkin' 'bout later, after we get settled someplace where no one's lookin' for us and no one knows who we are. Looks like we're gonna be together from now on. Might as well make it legal."

Dawn liked hearing him say that they were going to be together. But his last comment amused her. "Seems funny to hear you talk about anything legal."

Walt snickered. "Well, Dawn, maybe you said it yourself that last night we was campin' out."

Dawn glanced at him, not sure what exactly he was referring to.

"Reckon I do got what you'd call a romantic side," Walt offered. He lifted his gloved hand from the pommel of his saddle and scratched a pretend itch on the side of his face, adding: "'Least when it comes to some things."

"Like marriage?" Dawn asked slyly, with a cock of her head.

Walt took a long time answering. Finally he said: "Why not? Admit I never gave it much thought before. Then I never met anyone I'd wanta be settled with. I knowed lotsa gals, sure. But they was just for havin' a good time. Nothin' serious."

"I'm sure you must have been quite a ladies' man," Dawn remarked teasingly.

Walt shrugged. "Suppose." He rode on quietly a little farther. And then he said: "Fact is, I ain't never met no one like you. Had a lot of time to think, Dawn, sittin' inside that jail cell. Keepin' thoughts of you in my head helped me not to dwell on . . . well, other things. Anyway, I . . ." His words faded off into silence.

Dawn too remained quiet. She was curious to hear him out. More than curious. She was eager that what he might finish saying would be the words she was hoping for.

Walt shifted his position on the saddle a couple of times. "Well, Dawn, the truth is . . . I've gotten to be quite fond of you." He halted, scrunched up his face in deliberation, then blurted: "Hell, I've fallen in love with you."

Dawn did not try to resist the broadening smile that crossed her lips. Though she still didn't speak.

Walt seemed flustered by her silence. "Well, ain't you gonna say somethin'?" he snapped.

Dawn drew a deep breath of the dry desert air. She spoke quietly, phrasing her words so that her reply was proper. "I've been trying to tell you how I felt for a long time, Walt. Never seemed right, though . . . since I wasn't sure about your feelings."

"Reckon I knew even then," Walt admitted. "But it just wasn't right at the time."

"No," Dawn said with a sigh. "I suppose it wasn't."

"Time's gotta matter now, though," Walt added. "I don't wanta be wastin' any of what I got left." He paused momentarily. "Y'know, Dawn, I'd hate to think what you done back there in Colfax was just 'cause you felt pity for me."

"No, it wasn't pity," Dawn assured him. " 'Course I didn't want to see you hang. But . . . no . . ."

"Well," Walt said with a satisfied smile, "I reckon that's settled then."

Dawn's heart beat a little faster.

"But," she said hesitantly, "there *is* one thing I haven't been completely honest about."

Now it was Walt's turn to appear curious.

"My name," she said. "It isn't really Dawn."

"No?"

"Well, it's part of my name. My middle name and the one I chose to have people call me by. But it's really . . . Montana."

A wide grin swept across Walt's features. Before Dawn could think he was about to break into laughter, Walt nodded his head agreeably and said: "Montana. That—that's a right fine name."

Dawn explained to him how she had come to be named Montana . . . and then with all seriousness made Walt promise just to keep calling her Dawn. He told her he would, though he said

Montana was just about the best name he had ever heard.

Later, as they rode through a sun drenched midafternoon, Walt said: "I been figgerin' our options. As I see it, our best chance is to veer south."

"South? They'll be looking for you there," Dawn countered.

"They're lookin' for me everywhere, Dawn," Walt reminded, his tone easy. "More rightly, now they're lookin' for *us*. Goin' south is our best prospect. Unlikely we'll run into any riders. They knew we was in California. Also there was that stage job we pulled up in Reno. The way I see it, if we can cross the border into Mexico we might have a chance."

"I suppose," Dawn said with a thoughtful expression.

Walt glanced skyward, squinting against the blaze of the sun. "'Course we do got us one problem."

Dawn looked at him with a questioning expression.

Walt turned to her and both his face and voice were grave. "No cash. We're gonna need us a stake. I only got a few dollars from that deputy. And you ain't got that money I gave you."

"They found it as soon as they found me," Dawn explained.

"Probably went right into Collins' pocket too."

Walt coughed deliberately. "Yeh, and I guess I should be apologizin' for leavin' you like I did."

"No. I know why you did it," Dawn said honestly.

"Well . . . that's good. Just hadda know you was gonna be safe."

"Being safe isn't as important to me as being with you, Walt," Dawn declared.

"Well, you are now." Walt chuckled, adding with a teasing lift of an eyebrow: "For better or worse. But we do gotta get us some money," he said again.

Walt didn't have to elaborate. Dawn knew what he was saying. There was only the one way he could get some quick money. The only way he knew how.

Walt kept his eyes steady on her, waiting to see if she would object. But the girl neither presented an expression nor uttered a sound to either protest—or encourage.

He spoke to reassure her. "Just this one, Dawn. Enough to get us that stake. Then we'll move on and try to . . . try to set up that life you talked 'bout."

"I suppose . . . there isn't any other way?" she said.

"There ain't, Dawn," Walt told her outright.

Dawn knew it wouldn't do any good to try and talk him out of what he was proposing. And after contemplation she had to admit that Walt had the only answer. They would need money. And she could not think of another solution.

"Sure, there's a risk," Walt admitted. "But if you look at it, I'm takin' a risk every minute I try to keep free. They're huntin' for us right now, you can be sure of that. And they ain't gonna be too particular how they get me. Fact is, I've already been tried and found guilty, so there ain't the need to bring me in no other way than dead."

"Please, Walt, don't talk that way," Dawn pleaded.

Walt saw how his words had upset her. But since she'd made the choice to be with him, had taken her own risks, he felt that he had to be upfront with her.

But what he wouldn't tell her was his own certainty that their chances of escaping to that "better life" were slim.

"Nothin' worse can happen to me, Dawn, you know that. All I gotta concern myself with is takin' the money and gettin' away clean." He tossed a wink at her to punctuate his confidence. "And it ain't like I never robbed a bank before. Do got some skill in that profession."

Dawn nodded and tried to look agreeable to Walt's plan. But she knew she wasn't succeeding very well.

They continued riding at a leisurely pace to prevent their horses from getting thirsty while the sun was peaked. They had to be prudent with their water supply. But after a while Walt felt they were traveling too slow.

"We'd better pick up some speed 'fore nightfall," he said. "Gonna have to find a place to camp and try and get some shut eye. There's a little spit-in-the-mud town just beyond the hills called Eagle Breach, with a bank I'd like to reach by late afternoon tomorrow. Best time, after the day's deposits have been made."

Dawn was silent. Uncertain, as only a woman watching her man take such a gamble could be. But she was with him now.

And she would ride into Hell with him, if need be.

More humiliation awaited Deputy Blackie Collins when the hanging party arrived at the sheriff's office at dawn and he had to stand with his back to the bars while the kerchief was untied from his mouth so that he could tell them where the spare key ring to the jail was kept since Walt Egan had taken the original set. With the gag removed, Collins instantly spit out a tooth broken by Walt's blow that had been floating around in his bloody mouth all night.

When the men had entered the office they were aghast to find Collins locked in the cell with Egan gone. Collins wasted no time explaining what happened. He told his story carefully, and with much difficulty due to the injury to his jaw, which radiated pain all along the left side of his face. It was imperative that he make Judge Reynolds and the others understand he was not at fault, that he'd been cleverly and deviously tricked. The men listened, their expressions fixed, not revealing whether they were convinced or doubtful of his claim. Collins threw any responsibility off himself when he informed Judge Reynolds directly that it was Dawn Harley who was responsible for Egan's escape. The girl whom the judge had chosen to go easy on.

Collins winced as he lightly pressed the palm of his hand against his tender jaw. "What more proof do you need, Judge?" he slurred, his tone almost accusatory. "Whether she pulled the trigger or not, I think we know now that she had as much to do with Jed Harley's murder as Egan."

The judge was at a loss to defend his position. The stern look on his face became one of regret as he realized that he had indeed been wrong about the girl. He had to believe Collins' story since there was no other logical way the jailbreak could have happened. Still, he felt a silent sorrow, not only because he had misjudged Dawn, but through her action she had almost admitted her complicity in the murder of her husband, and had now made herself a fugitive.

The judge suggested that Collins have Doc Speer take a look at him, to check if his jaw was indeed broken.

"If it was, I wouldn't be able to be talkin'," Collins argued. Much of what he spoke was garbled.

"You're not doing so well now," the judge observed.

But the deputy insisted he was fine. He wasn't; he was hurting bad, but remained adamant. Just as he was determined to ride with the posse to go after Walt Egan and Dawn Harley. Much to his pleasure, not only was his demand granted, he was again given charge of the riders, though the judge made it clear his decision was based on getting the men on the trail quickly and Collins was still the only man in town with a badge. There was a further stipulation: The judge would be riding with them. This was not at all to Collins' liking. The judge's presence would ensure that everything would be done legally. This time the deputy had wanted to deal with the outlaws his own way. He was hoping to bring Walt Egan and possibly Dawn Harley back to town with their bodies draped over their saddles.

But Collins worked quickly. He gathered up the men who had rode with him on the first posse, plus some extra volunteers. He immediately dispatched a man to ride out and obtain the services of an ancient named Will Philpott, who was an experienced tracker but who had recently been laid up in bed with a lingering fever. As long as he wasn't dying and could ride a horse

Collins wanted Philpott with them. Fortunately the old man was up and around and eager to join them in their hunt.

Eighteen men were assembled within the hour. This time it was decided that a large number of men would be needed. With his head already in a noose, Egan was sure to be desperate to avoid a second capture. Plus he was riding with an accomplice who, female or not, had proven herself just as cunning and potentially dangerous as he was.

They got lucky when a vigilant citizen came forward and informed them that he saw two people leave town the night before, riding in a southerly direction. Though it was dark, he claimed to be certain that one was a female.

The men mounted their horses and rode out, leaving a trail of dust in their wake.

CHAPTER ELEVEN

It was sundown by the time Dawn and Walt reached the rocky foothills. Both were exhausted from riding all day without rest. Dawn had prepared for what she had expected to be a long ride by padding her bottom and bringing along a pair of her husband's chaps so that she wouldn't get sore on the saddle. Walt had no such protection, not even riding chaps, but he never once expressed discomfort. Dawn marveled at his stamina and figured that he'd either developed tough callouses from all the riding he'd done through the years or simply had a high threshold for pain.

They followed a narrow path alongside the north slopes until Walt finally noticed a ridge high up in the hills that they could access by horseback. They couldn't chance leaving their horses behind at a distance while they made the climb on foot. The animals were likewise tired from their ceaseless day of riding under the hot sun and Walt had to urge his temperamental mount up the incline, carefully followed by Dawn. Finally they reached the summit and settled into a stony hollow. Protected by perched boulders on the eastern and western sides, it looked like a safe and practical place to set up camp. Walt wasn't too concerned about any approach from the south, but he wanted an unimpeded view of whoever might be coming from the north.

When Walt announced that it wouldn't be smart for them to build a fire, Dawn realized with alarm that she had forgotten to bring along extra blankets. They also did not have bedrolls. Without a fire there would be no protection against the cold.

And that presented a problem since temperatures were sure to dip low throughout the night. Walt looked momentarily disappointed at her oversight but could not be upset as he considered all of the other preparations Dawn had to contend with getting him out of jail. But now, out of necessity, he would have to make that fire and he didn't find the idea to his liking. The spot they'd chosen provided good cover but there was a lot of open country around them and the glow of a campfire in the night darkness, however faint, along with the smoke that might billow forth like an Indian smoke signal would almost certainly be noticed by trackers.

Walt's only option was to keep the fire burning low. He went about collecting some dry shrubbery while Dawn removed the gear from the horses and started setting up their supper. Walt built a small campfire and afterward the two consumed the meal that Dawn had brought along. For dessert Dawn had prepared a special surprise. She'd baked an apple pie at home, which she'd cut into slices for their travel. Of course the pie was quite soggy after the day's hot ride, but it still tasted delicious to Walt and he devoured two pieces with gusto.

When they were done eating, Dawn opened her sack and began pulling out provisions she'd packed for Walt. She removed each item with delight, as if she were displaying Christmas gifts. There was a cake of soap, Jed's razor, and shaving glass. Even a small unopened bottle of brandy, which Dawn explained should help keep them warm. Walt's eyes widened with pleasure at that last item and he hastened to treat himself to a generous swallow. He smacked his lips and gave his head a satisfied nudge. He handed the bottle to Dawn who just took a few tentative, delicate sips, reacting sourly to the strong, burning taste. Walt felt no restraint and by the time he had half finished the brandy he was feeling quite mellow.

He relaxed with his back resting against the smooth edge of a boulder.

"Considerate of you to bring along that stuff."

"Knew you'd be needing a few things," Dawn merely said.

Walt coughed. "Don't wanta sound like I'm complainin', but there are a coupla things you forgot that I sure could use right 'bout now."

"What's that?" Dawn asked, her expression curious.

Walt tilted his head back and spoke longingly. "Yeh, some papers and a pouch of tobacco."

Dawn was apologetic. "I—never even thought . . ."

Walt returned from his momentary reverie. "No matter," he said with a shrug. "By the way, didn't you bring anything along for yourself?" he wanted to know.

"A hairbrush," Dawn answered. "And some other things."

Walt looked regretful. "You know, if I coulda held onto some of that money, know what I'd do? Buy you all the fancy dresses you could wear. Yeh, and some jewelry and perfume. All the fancy things a gal like you deserves. You wouldn't want for nothin'."

"I don't need any fancy things," Dawn said dismissively. "I've got all that's necessary. Just a few items to make a woman feel pretty."

Walt gazed at her. "As far as I'm concerned, you don't need nothin' special to make you purty, Dawn."

Dawn flicked her eyes to the side with modesty. "I've never really thought of myself as particularly attractive," she said.

"Sure you are," Walt said enthusiastically. "Attractive . . . and you got some smarts too. Can tell by the way you talk. Musta had some schooling."

Dawn nodded, her thoughts traveling back to memories of Montana. "Did go to school for a while. But most of my learning came from books. I always liked to read."

Walt chuckled, a little self-consciously. "That's what I mean. You're educated. Me—I never saw the inside of a classroom. And I guess the only thing I ever learned to read was the dollar value of currency. Reckon in my line that's about all I really need to know."

"Maybe—I could teach you someday," Dawn offered tentatively, so as not to embarrass or offend him.

Walt considered the proposition. Then he rocked his head. "Maybe."

Afterward, they huddled together close to the fire's crackling warmth. Walt opened the flap of his duster and Dawn slid inside and he wrapped the flap around her. She loved being so near to Walt, and in every way it fulfilled her fantasy of how it would feel to be held in his arms. She snuggled up tighter to him, pressing her body into his, pretending to seek more warmth but wanting only to get as physically close to him as she could. Walt flexed his forearm and strengthened his grip around her shoulders and hugged her. Dawn sighed contentedly and lifted her face toward his. With the glow of the flames flashing against her features, highlighting the perfect contours, she was an almost ethereal image. Walt removed the battered old hat she was wearing and began to undo the ribbon with which she had tied back her hair. As the strawberry blonde locks were freed and flowing he tenderly brushed the hair down over her shoulders.

He was overcome with true admiration. "My God, Dawn, you *are* a right fine-lookin' girl."

It was as if he was seeing her for the first time; reacting like he'd been struck by a thunderbolt.

He half-shifted his upper body, and he bent forward to kiss her. She met his lips eagerly and both immediately gave in to their passion, releasing all the emotion they'd held for each other in the exchange of brandy-flavored kisses. His lips blazed across her mouth and she responded in kind. Walt's kiss was as powerful as he was a man, and Dawn delighted in it. She'd never been kissed with such a strong desire. The almost-forgotten kisses she'd gotten from Jed had never stimulated her the way she felt having Walt's lips pressed against hers. Suddenly her body was flooded with a different kind of warmth. A wondrous, consuming, almost intoxicating warmth that came from within. Walt had his hand pressed against her chest and could feel how rapidly her heart was beating. His own heart was thumping just as fast.

When after many minutes they finally pulled their lips part, Dawn took a moment to sit in silence. Then she sighed, smiled up at him a little sadly, and said: "I don't think I've ever been this happy. And yet . . ." Her words drifted off.

Walt knew what it was that she couldn't finish saying. After all, he reasoned, she was a woman and prone to the doubts and uncertainties that a man would often ignore. He wanted to reassure her, even if he had a more pragmatic view of the outcome.

"I know, girl," he said. "But we're free now and if we're careful we can stay that way."

Dawn looked at him hopefully, her doe-like chestnut eyes riveted on his so firmly and completely that not even the approach of a posse could have maneuvered them away.

"Do you really think that, Walt?"

Walt drew his lips together and gave his head a definite nod. "I *do*," he said firmly. He elaborated. "And you wanta know why? 'Cause I don't believe we was brought together just to be pulled apart."

Dawn appreciated hearing these words and the conviction with which Walt spoke them. It gave her renewed strength and a continued optimism.

Walt went on. "I ain't by no means what you'd call a religious man. But I do believe that things happen for a purpose. Like my meetin' you. Then all that happened . . . with Jed—and Sam. Then my leavin' you, never thinkin' I'd see you agin.

But look how things turned out. In a kinda strange way, I grant you. But it was meant to be, Dawn. As simple as that."

Dawn cast her eyes toward the weakening flames of the campfire. She further absorbed what Walt was saying—understanding about fate or destiny, or whatever one chose to call that dictating force. She rocked her head slowly, acknowledging the truth in Walt's words. They *were* brought together for a reason, and it was wrong to believe that whatever this power was . . . that it could be so cruel to separate them after all they'd overcome to share a future together.

She was reluctant to let Walt pull away from her when he started to get up to throw more shrubbery onto the fire to keep it burning just enough and to keep the plumes of smoke at a minimum. She never wanted to be free of his embrace. She felt that as long as she could touch him, feel him, no harm would come to him. Maybe that was a crazy way to be thinking, but Dawn didn't believe so. She loved Walt with a profoundness she could never have imagined and just wanted to protect him. She determined that she would—in any way necessary.

To protect him, love him, and be with him forever—that was all she wanted. Was that too much to ask? It was a silent pleading, speaking to whoever . . . or whatever it was that controlled their destinies.

Finally all the emotion she had been with-holding gave way and she started to sob. As tears ran down her cheeks, Walt looked at her, perplexed, and unsure of how to respond. He wasn't used to seeing a woman cry. Most of the girls he had known were as hard-edged as him. They wouldn't shed tears if their own mother died. He said nothing, just sat back beside her and wrapped his arms around her while she laid her head against his shoulder and let the tears run freely.

"Why're you cryin'?" he asked her.

"I just want us to always be together," she said. "Like it is now."

"We will be, Dawn," Walt said comfortingly. "And look . . . even if the worst should happen, we got what we have here and now."

Dawn glanced up at him, her eyes puddles of moisture. "Is it selfish of me to think that's not enough?" she asked with a sniffle.

Walt smiled. "'Course not. Reckon I feel the same. But right now I'm just happy for every minute I can be with you."

"Happy," Dawn echoed in a sigh. "I'm—glad to hear you say that."

"Well," Walt drew out, "just don't you ever be doubtin' it."

Dawn was starting to feel better, but was now embarrassed at exposing emotions she tried to keep guarded. She wiped under her eyes and spoke apologetically. "I'm sorry. I don't know why—"

Walt shushed her. "Don't go feelin' bad 'bout it," he told her. "You been through a lot. Don't know if a man coulda handled all you done. Or done as well." He looked fully into her face. "Yeh, you're quite a gal, Dawn."

Dawn's expression suddenly twisted in a slight grimace. Walt asked her if she was all right.

"Just a bit of a headache," she replied. "Must be from drinking that brandy."

Walt's eyes widened. "Just those few sips?"

"I've never drank alcohol before," Dawn confessed sheepishly.

Walt gave her a strange look. He'd met few women in his travels who couldn't drink as much as him—or handle it as well. He found Dawn's aversion to alcohol a refreshing change. Without uttering a word, he positioned himself behind her, removed his black riding gloves, and began massaging her temples with his fingertips. Dawn closed her eyes as they touched and let out a sigh. His fingers were long and surprisingly smooth and she tingled as she felt the gentle pressure of their rotation against her skin. Her head lolled as she relaxed and the ache started to fade and she became drowsy.

Soon she drifted off to slumber and Walt edged back beside her, gently wrapping her inside the fold of his duster and held her in his embrace throughout the long, cold night. He remained alert and would not waken her to take a watch while he collected himself some shut-eye. He could probably use a few hours for what he was planning tomorrow, but he'd trained himself to get by with little or no sleep. He could recall times when he'd gone for almost a full week without closing his eyes. Besides, he felt content and rested in his own way, and enjoyed holding Dawn and watching her while she slept. He was captivated by her loveliness, her face especially soft and peaceful in repose—a beauty that he'd never taken the time to notice before.

For a man hardened by life experiences and corrupted by the path that he himself had chosen, Walt could finally know in full the one emotion that had been foreign to him: He was in love.

"Damn, if that ain't somethin'," he marveled.

The posse had ridden all day, with only brief, periodic rest and watering breaks, and kept on the trail into the night. Old Will Philpott, the tracker, was good at his work and had picked up the pair's direction early on. He remarked that it was a safe bet given their eastward movement that they would head into the Grady Hills. At the pace they were maintaining the posse intended to reach that destination before sunup.

"Gotta lot of ground to cover in those hills," Blackie Collins said, his speech still slurred through the swollen puffiness of his jaw. "And if

194

they're in there, it's a good bet they'll spot us comin'."

"Let 'em spot us," toothless old Will Philpott challenged. "As long as they don't start takin' no potshots at us from any of them ridges, we'll soon enough get 'em cornered. Know them hills pretty well."

"He'd have a good chance takin' long-range potshots with that Winchester he took," Collins said with a frown.

Judge Reynolds overheard what the pair was saying and rode up alongside them. "Think it's wise to go in when it's dark?" he asked. "Won't that give them the advantage?"

Collins had to keep from rolling his eyes. The judge had no business coming along with the posse. He knew nothing about how a manhunt was conducted. Or that chasing someone like Walt Egan had definite risks. But he kept his mouth shut and let Will Philpott do the explaining.

"Less chance of 'em seein' us if we come round when it's still dark," Will said patiently. " 'Specially if we separate into smaller groups and come in from different directions. Also a good idea if we send along some men to keep watch at the southern base. A lot of distance to scout, but it's wide-open country on either side so unless they sneak out under cover of night, shouldn't be hard to spot."

The judge seemed satisfied. Will Philpott had been tracking almost from the time he could walk. He'd learned his technique from the Navajos, yet, ironically, had later been hired by the government to scout for cavalry troops in the Southwest who were commanded to track so-called renegade bands whose only crime was to hold onto the land that was rightfully theirs. Of course many people didn't look at it that way.

Expansion into these territories was considered progress. But Judge Reynolds was a liberal thinker and secretly had a great respect for the Indians.

The judge noticed how Collins was still experiencing discomfort each time he worked his jaw and how swollen and discolored the left side of his face had become.

Finally he spoke with almost paternal concern. "Collins, I think I made a mistake letting you come along. Doc Speer should have taken a look at you first, in case your jaw needs mending. I'm not knowledgeable when it comes to medical matters, but I don't need to be a doctor to tell you I don't like the look of that swelling."

Collins appeared uninterested in the judge's caring. He believed he was merely trying to make amends for the guilt he felt for being wrong about Dawn Harley.

"You don't want to end up with something permanent—or worse." The judge went on, "An injury like that might even lead to infection. Then you've got troubles."

"I been hit in the face harder than what Egan done to me, Judge," Collins replied with bravado. "It's sore, but it'll heal." He paused, then finally admitted the truth. " 'Sides, you might as well be knowin' I've got me a grudge to settle."

Judge Reynolds nodded slowly. "I figured as much. But the way you explained it, Collins, no one can hold you responsible for what happened back in Colfax. If I'd been in the jailhouse and Dawn Harley had walked in, I'd have been tricked just as easily. Hard thing to own up to, but I misplaced my faith in her."

"'Preciate that, Judge," Collins said, with no feeling of genuine gratitude. After all, Reynolds wasn't crediting Collins for having been right all along.

"The point is, Collins, don't let plain stubbornness jeopardize your well being. We'll get Egan and the girl, no doubt about that. Getting your health back if you're ignoring something that needs attention . . . well, that isn't so sure."

"Sorry, Judge," Collins said with firmness, without looking at him. "I ain't turnin' back now. Not 'til we finish this."

Judge Reynolds nodded, but his nod was doubtful. He turned his head away and gave it a quick shake. His main worry was that if a serious problem should develop with the deputy, they were miles away from any help.

When the judge was not looking Collins expectorated off to his side. He was dismayed to see that there was still a generous amount of blood in his spittle. He'd been tasting copper and spitting out blood throughout the ride but had thought it was only an aftereffect. The blood he'd noticed before hadn't been much, but what he saw this time was almost pure red.

Still, he just sat himself firmly on his saddle and rode on.

The darkness started to worry Walt and he began to grow restless. He'd calculated how long it should take the posse from Colfax to get on his trail, if they followed the correct direction, and within that estimated time frame, which included the discovery of his escape and the assembling of men, he'd felt comfortable stopping for a rest break. But before long, sitting alone in the quiet and the dark, he fell prey to his thoughts and decided to wake Dawn and get them on their way.

He aroused Dawn gingerly so as not to startle her and get her to worrying that they were in immediate danger. He explained calmly that it was best that they move out while it was still dark so that they could have a good start before sunup. Walt extinguished the fire and kicked dirt around it to prevent smoldering. Then they packed their horses and navigated their mounts with caution down the rocky incline of the ridge, following the same path on which they'd traveled up, with only the illumination of the full autumn moon as their guide. Walt took the lead and told Dawn to follow his course precisely.

"Ride slow, Dawn," he instructed the girl, speaking over his shoulder. "No need to hurry. Misstep now and we'll pay for it later."

Dawn heeded his advice, but to her it was a long ride down. She firmly held onto the reins with both hands. She was still not entirely comfortable atop a horse, particularly on such tricky terrain, loose with gravel and bits of stony rubble.

When they finally reached safer and more level ground, Walt backed his horse alongside Dawn and told the nervous girl that she had done fine.

They started a brisker ride out of the slopes and the wider ridges of the hills. Walt was hoping that if the posse followed their trail they'd scout out the hill range. They might find that they'd been there, but the search would delay them and give Dawn and him several extra hours, if not longer, to maintain their distance.

And that was important because he still had that next day's stopover in the town of Eagle Breach.

CHAPTER TWELVE

Deputy Blackie Collins had begun to sway on the saddle. Though he tried to keep erect he was feeling dizzy—and fevered. It had been coming upon him gradually during the last hour or so of his ride, but now the sickness hit him with a vengeance. He was finding it increasingly difficult both to maintain his balance and control his mount. He found this frustrating since he'd been on horses all his life.

But he carried on, summoning all the fortitude he could manage so that no one else might notice what was happening with him. Especially Judge Reynolds. Collins resented that old fool almost as much as he had Henry Thornton. If Reynolds had followed his advice Egan would be hanged by now, Dawn Harley locked in a jail cell, and instead of suffering on another posse he'd be receiving his appointment as marshal of Colfax.

Fortunately it was dark. Each of the men appeared as a shadow, some as flowing, batlike forms since the desert winds had picked up a little and most wore dusters as protection against the cold. If anyone noticed anything different about the way Collins was riding they'd likely think he was just tired after the long day's ride. They were all bone-tired and they still had to reach the hills. The peaks were visible on the horizon, reflecting silver under the bright moon-glow. Another few hours and they would be entering the foothills, reaching their destination by sunup, just as they'd planned.

Then would come the hard part—trekking through treacherous terrain and trying to keep out of the range of Egan's gunsight. Normally this wouldn't be a concern; Collins had welcomed the opportunity to get his chance at the outlaw. But now he was at a severe disadvantage.

Collins had been determined to see this through. Now he was starting to have doubt. Serious doubt. He was still tasting and spitting out globs of blood and was sick to his stomach. He began to pull back, gradually, so that the other riders would move ahead of him.

Soon he had to acknowledge that he simply could not go on. He pulled at the reins and drew his horse to a halt. No one in the posse noticed as they moved farther ahead, vanishing from his sight, absorbed into the night.

Collins reached for his canteen, twisted open the cap, but was suddenly so weak that the canteen dropped from his fingers, his water spilling into the sand. He needed help bad but didn't have the strength to call out. Blood had began seeping from his mouth. He feared he was hemorrhaging. He went for his gun, slowly pulled it free of his holster, raised it . . . and using the few ounces of energy remaining to him, pulled the trigger. The report echoed in the desert stillness. The last thing Blackie Collins heard was someone call out in the distance . . . before he toppled from his saddle face first into the sand.

They rode through the dark and were back on the flatlands by daybreak. Now traveling by the sun's early light, Walt frequently searched back over his shoulder as they gained ground farther from the hills. There was no sign of any pursuers. He suddenly felt lucky and told Dawn that he had a good feeling about the day's outcome.

Dawn, of course, was still doubtful, though she maintained a somewhat optimistic expression.

Walt said: "By the way, Dawn, I been meanin' to ask you 'bout that gun."

"Gun?"

"Yeah, the Navy Colt you used to break me outta jail."

"Oh." Dawn seemed a little reluctant to explain. "It—it was Jed's."

"That so?" Walt said, nodding his head. "So all that time ol' Jed did have a weapon handy."

"He kept it locked away. He never would have used it."

"No, I reckon he wouldn't." Walt took a pause. "How 'bout you?"

Dawn thought about her answer, carefully. It was a question she had never really considered.

"When I knew I'd be coming for you I did some practice. I never held a gun before in my life. Don't know if I would have—or *could* have—shot the deputy, if it had come to that. I'm just glad I didn't have to make that decision."

Walt seemed impressed. "Just scare him, huh? Well, you played your cards right, girl. Would hate for them to hang a killing on you. 'Specially a lawman."

Dawn considered a little longer. "But I think I could have," she then said.

"Better you didn't find out," Walt commented. "Not the most reliable handgun, even if Wild Bill preferred it."

"Wild Bill?" Dawn questioned.

"Hickock," Walt clarified. "He was a gunfighter and lawman . . .'til he got a bullet in the back of the head while playin' cards. Anyway, the Navy Colt was his gun of choice. For myself . . . would never carry a single-action revolver. Good only as a souvenir."

Walt rode on quietly a little farther. Dawn could tell by the studied look on his face that his brain was working.

Come daylight, three men, including Judge Reynolds, were left behind to bury Blackie Collins while Will Philpott had led the rest of the posse toward the Grady Hills. Time was still important. The three men would catch up later.

After the sandy grave was dug and Collins interred, one of the posse, Kent James, sidled up next to the judge.

"How d'you see it, Judge? Another murder?"

"Don't see what difference that makes," Judge Reynolds replied, his eyes focused on the mound of sand covering the deputy. "The rope's still waiting for Egan. But the fact is, Collins brought this upon himself by being so mule-headed stubborn."

"Far as I'm concerned, hangin's too good for Egan," Kent said through his teeth. "Killin', robbin', horse thief." He shook his head and spoke less agressively. "Funny, never much cared for Collins. But now I think he woulda made a fine marshal. He sure was set on bringin' them two in."

The judge nodded solemnly. "So much that it killed him."

A small rise overlooked the town of Eagle Breach. The isolated town was nestled between the rolling hills and from their vantage point appeared as a populated indentation against the frontier landscape. Walt and Dawn sat on their horses observing the small country community in silence. Both wore sober expressions.

Finally Walt said: "Sure won't get rich robbin' that bank, but it'll get us a few dollars."

Dawn sighed heavily. Walt turned to her.

"I just wish that it were over," she said. "And that we were on our way to Mexico."

"Won't be long, Dawn," Walt promised her.

In an attempt to ease her doubts and get her mind off what was ahead, Dawn asked: "What's Mexico like?"

Walt understood and obliged her. "Depends where you are," he said. "Like anywhere, I reckon, some places are nicer than others. But where I'd like for us to settle is Durango. Beautiful country, Dawn. Been there only once —oh, maybe 'bout seven, eight years ago. But I wouldn't suppose it's changed much." He tilted his head back, closed his eyes, and spoke with a clear reflection of his memories. "What I remember most are the mountains and green hills. And green like you never seen it. Lush, like a jewel. There's mountains, plenty of rivers and trees. 'Bout as close as you can get to paradise. Means more travel south, but once we get there we could find a place and live our lives without anyone ever knowin' who we are. If it came down to it, I could maybe find work on a ranch 'til we build enough of a stake to build our own place. Yeah, mighty fine country. Reckon the only thing we'd have to worry 'bout are the scorpions."

Dawn reacted with horror. *"Scorpions?"*

Walt nodded, quietly amused at her sequeamishness. "In fact, the Mexicans themselves call the people of Durango *Alacrán de Durango. Alacrán* is their word for scorpion."

"No matter what they call it, don't know if I like the idea of scorpions," Dawn said with a grimace.

"Just gotta be watchful. 'Sides, where we been ridin' ain't been free of critters. We've just been lucky not to run into any of 'em."

"I—suppose," Dawn said timidly.

Walt continued. "They have a church there. Called the Cathedral Church. Be a fine place for us to get married."

"Walt, you make it sound so wonderful," Dawn said dreamily, entranced by the picture, then suddenly shifting her expression. "Except for the scorpions."

"It's gonna be, Dawn. Once I finish up here," Walt said, looking skyward to the position of the sun. "We still got us 'bout an hour. "The way I got this timed, even if they send men after us we should be able to lose 'em in the dark, hidin' out in the hills."

He noticed the worry once more start to creep across Dawn's features and again tried to reassure her.

"The take's gonna be small but so's the risk. One lawman and a community full of yokels. We'll be raisin' dust 'fore they even know what hit 'em."

"And—what do you want me to do?" Dawn asked tentatively.

"Just ride through." Walt scouted the outcropping of hills opposite the town and pointed toward a southern hillcrest bordered by clusters of large rock. "Head to that ridge on the other side. Maybe tuck your hair up under your hat. Better if no one in town don't recognize you as a female. Just be waitin'. Looks like 'bout a mile or so ride, but you should have plenty of time. And once you hear me fire my gun that'll mean I'm outta the bank and you start ridin' like the devil. Don't worry 'bout waitin' for me. I'll catch up."

Dawn started to bundle her long strawberry blonde hair into the hollow of her Stetson. Walt watched her with a pleased expression.

"Damn honey, ain't no way anyone with eyes could ever mistake you for a man," he said with a burst of emphasis. "But I guess that'll have to do. Just don't ride too slow and don't go lookin' direct at no one."

Dawn smiled demurely but appreciatively at the compliment.

"How long do you think it will take—the bank, I mean?" she asked.

"Probably not more'n a few minutes," Walt answered with a shrug. "First, I'm gonna ride in and do a bit of scoutin'; see how things look. Gimme 'bout ten minutes, then you follow and just ride on through."

They sat on their mounts for a few moments

longer, both with their own thoughts. Then Walt turned to Dawn and said: "Okay, I'm set."

Before he could start to ride, Dawn leaned over and planted a kiss on his bristled cheek. She wanted to wrap her arms around him, embrace him, and physically keep him from going. At that moment she would have done almost anything to stop him. But nothing was going to deter Walt, and she didn't want him to pursue his course accompanied by the worry of her own apprehension.

"Everything's gonna be fine," he said, taking her hand and giving it a squeeze. "Just keep thinkin' 'bout us in Mexico."

He absorbed a long, final look of her and then gently urged his horse down the hill toward Eagle Breach.

Dawn's eyes stayed on him as she watched him go. Soon he was riding down the main street of the town. She waited the ten minutes he suggested . . . and started down the slope.

But as she rode a gnawing anxiety began to take hold of her—a sudden feeling of dread at what Walt was about to do. As much as she tried to find comfort in his repeated assurances, she could not ignore this penetrating grip of foreboding.

She would protect her man even if she had to ride into Hell to do it.

She'd made that promise to herself. And now she found herself struggling with an urge that in some ways made no logical sense to her, but one that quickly culminated in her decision to disappoint Walt. . . .

What a meager little town, Walt thought glumly as his horse clip-clopped down the dirt road along Eagle Breach's main street. He briefly reflected on the days when he rode with the Chancer Gang and how they never would have bothered with such a town—not even to scoop up some quick saloon money. He'd be lucky to see a couple hundred bucks for his effort.

The one thing he felt quite confident of was that he shouldn't run into any trouble. The few citizens he saw scattered about the street did not look like the type to put up a fight.

But he reminded himself of how he had also underestimated Barron Creek.

Walt rode through the street only once before reining his horse into a turn and going back around. People noticed him, but not with any specific interest. Eagle Breach frequently served as a stopover for travelers heading north or south and could even boast its own stagecoach station, which provided passengers with a rest stop and a nearby restaurant for meals. Strangers were common here.

Walt considered the few dollars he had taken from Deputy Blackie Collins and decided to spend the money on a small cloth sack in which to hold the bank take and also a couple of blankets at the dry-goods store. He and Dawn would be camping out for a while yet and would need the extra warmth at night until they got far enough south. He made the purchase and, after packing the blankets onto his horse, went into the restaurant for a cup of coffee. Even though the afternoon was warm he kept his duster on, to conceal his gunbelt. He sat at a table next to the window that overlooked the street where he could notice Dawn once she rode through on her way to the ridge. He didn't fear being recognized in such a remote community, but still wore the brim of his Stetson low and had several days' growth of beard to further disguise him. Rubbing his hand along the roughness of his face, he thought about how good a wash and shave would feel and decided to make that his first priority once they were far away and he and Dawn could settle down for a spell.

He drank his coffee slowly and kept watch out the window. He began to grow concerned when he didn't see Dawn pass. If she had followed his instructions she would have come through by now.

Now worried and not a little impatient, Walt dropped the silver for his coffee onto the table and left the restaurant. He stood on the boardwalk gazing into the direction where Dawn was to come. No sign of her. He couldn't have missed her, he thought, unless she'd followed quicker and had somehow got by him when he was scouting the street.

Then—he turned and spotted her horse, fastened to the railing outside the Eagle Breach Commercial Bank. Puzzled, angry, he untied his horse and walked the animal the several yards toward the bank, looping the reins loosely around the post next to Dawn's mount.

Walt opened the flap of his duster and strode into the bank. He was glad to see that there were no customers present, but he immediately spotted the Stetson-wearing, buckskin clad figure of Dawn standing at one of the three wickets, chatting with a bank clerk. Walt suppressed a scowl. Dawn pretended to ignore him as he entered. But Walt noticed the clasp of her handbag was open and that she was holding the bag close in front of her, with her left hand poised above it. There was a clock on the wall. The Roman numerals read 3:15. The bank closed at 3:30.

In just those few seconds Walt guessed the purpose behind Dawn's presence in the bank. Why she had disobeyed his instructions. He didn't like it—but he could not let that interfere with his plans.

The clerk, a timid-looking, well dressed man, peered curiously at Walt over his rimless spectacles as he approached the wicket. He seemed to recognize that Walt was not a customer of the bank. In a town as small as Eagle Breach he would surely know all of the regular depositors.

"Good afternoon, sir. How may I help you?" he asked in a pleasant manner as he adjusted his spectacles.

Out the corner of her eye Dawn watched as Walt reached for the gun in his holster.

Walt offered a smile as he drew out his six-shooter and aimed it high and forward in a smooth, fluid movement. "You sure can, pardner," he said. "You can oblige me by emptying out your cash drawer."

Dawn immediately stepped back from the wicket and awkwardly pulled out the Navy Colt from her handbag, drawing the hammer back to full cock with her thumb.

"And nobody make a move—or else," she ordered the other two clerks, who stood motion-lessly behind their wickets. She gestured with her gun for them to raise their hands in the air.

Walt quickly flicked his eyes toward her and expelled a breath. God Almighty, she was coming across as a regular Belle Starr.

The timid bank clerk's own eyes darted from Walt to Dawn, then back again to Walt.

"Is this a holdup?" he asked over a lump in his throat.

Walt grinned and clicked the hammer on his revolver, pushing it up close to the clerk's face.

"Let's just call it a withdrawal," he said. "With a little persuasion."

"We've never been robbed before," the clerk said, a hint of excitement merging with the tremor in his voice.

Walt pulled the small sack from the pocket of his duster and thrust it at the clerk.

"Well then, friend, you're a part of history in the making. If you play it smart, could be one of the great moments of your life," he said lightly. Then he turned serious. "If not, I'll shoot you dead where you stand. Now start depositin' that money."

The bank manager was seated in an open cubicle off to the side. Dawn had him covered.

"Just stay put at your desk with your hands where I can see them," she said with a steely stare.

The manager obeyed, though his eyes shifted toward the top side drawer. There was only the one drawer on that side with an opening large enough for him to fit his leg underneath. The manager lifted his right knee unobtrusively and used it as a lever to slide the drawer open from the bottom. He maneuvered slowly, and with extreme caution so that the wood . . . wouldn't . . . creak.

Concealed inside was a derringer.

The timid clerk began pulling out all the bills he had in his cash drawer and placed the money into the cloth sack. Walt could tell that he had a great respect for money as he handled and deposited the currency carefully. As Walt had expected, there wasn't a lot of money, but after the clerk had emptied out all he had, Walt stepped over to the next teller and demanded the same cooperation. All the while Dawn stood aside covering the room with her Navy Colt. If she was nervous she certainly did not display it. Her gun hand was steady and her face was set and serious. Female or not, she had all of the bank employees convinced she was willing to shoot if they tried anything funny.

The sack was filled with folding money and some silver and the take looked small. Walt debated ordering the bank manager to open the safe. There had to be at least a few hundred extra dollars locked inside. But he decided against it, mainly because of Dawn. She'd handled herself fine, but he couldn't know how much longer she could hold up and didn't want to delay their exit out of town. As far as he was concerned, they'd been damn lucky, and he did not want to stretch their luck.

He started to back away from the wickets.

"Wanta thank you folks for your kind generosity," he said.

Dawn started to edge toward the door as well, moving in a careful sideways manner, her gun still trained on the employees.

The bank manager had the desk drawer opened

sufficiently to reach for the derringer. His hands were still raised high. . . . He knew he couldn't thrust a hand suddenly into the drawer; they'd be sure to notice such a move. His brain worked feverishly. He got an idea that could work. He faked a sneeze, dropping one of his hands toward his mouth as if in reflex—but then sweeping his fingers all the way downward to the open drawer, and making a grab for the gun. He leaped up from behind his desk brandishing the small weapon.

Walt was slow in noticing. But Dawn did.

Her eyes widened in panic. "Walt!" she cried.

Walt started to turn, but not fast enough. The bank manager fired off a quick shot. The bullet caught Walt in the upper arm, just below the shoulder. His gun hand dropped limply to his side, the revolver loose in his grip.

Taking swift aim, the Navy Colt clamped in both hands, Dawn squeezed her finger on the trigger. The gun exploded, she jerked back from the impact, and to her surprise and horror she saw the discharge strike the manager square in the chest. His body reeled backward, toppling over the swivel chair and landing dead on the floor behind it. The sole female clerk started to scream, growing to a hysterical pitch. Confused and dazed by her action, Dawn pivoted around to the woman, who stared into the barrel of the Colt and fainted dead away.

Walt shifted his revolver to his other hand and leveled it on the two tellers left standing. He looped his injured arm that was still gripping the sack around Dawn's waist and hastened her out of the bank. The gunshots and the girl teller's screams had alerted the attention of a few passersby outside who stood aside as Walt struggled onto his horse and Dawn climbed up on her mount. Walt fired a quick succession of shots as they raced off down the main street to discourage pursuit.

They made their getaway out of Eagle Breach, the citizens too frightened to follow, and rode with speed through the desert valley toward the southern hills.

And eventually Mexico.

CHAPTER THIRTEEN

They had no choice but to keep riding and they didn't stop until the sun went down and they were deep within the protection of the foothills. As it was, it could only be a brief stop, to rest the horses and examine Walt's injury.

It was pitch dark when they finally halted in among a large outcropping of rocks and Dawn had to scramble about collecting bits of shrubbery for burning. When she got a small fire started she had Walt lean in toward the glow so she could take a look at the severity of his wound. He was gritting his teeth and was in obvious pain.

"Wish I had me a cigarette," he said.

The arm of his shirt was bloody. Dawn carefully ripped open the fabric and tried not to wince as she gazed at the seeping wound. She did not know what to do. She'd never had to treat a gunshot.

"Bullet's still in there, Dawn, can feel it," Walt said tightly. "Was hopin' it woulda gone straight through."

Dawn looked at him, trying not to appear as helpless as she felt.

"Gonna have to dig it out," Walt told her. "It's deep agin the bone."

"You're—going to have to tell me what to do," Dawn said.

Walt grimaced as he nodded. "Need a knife. Somethin' sharp."

Dawn started to pale. "I—don't have anything like that."

"Yeh, I know," Walt said heavily. He looked at Dawn. "But you still got some of that brandy in your saddlebag?"

She nodded.

"Hate to waste good liquor, but you'd better pour some on that bullet hole. And maybe save a swallow for me."

Dawn rushed to her horse to fetch the brandy. There was less than half the bottle left. She opened the cap and knelt beside Walt.

"This is going to sting," she said.

Walt emittted an ironic laugh. "Yeh."

She steadied herself against the pain she knew Walt would experience and carefully poured some of the brandy directly into the wound. Walt had braced himself but still squirmed as the liquor seared into his arm.

After a few seconds he grabbed the bottle from her and gulped down what was remaining. He then tossed it aside and heard it shatter against the rocks. Walt tore off a piece of his ripped shirt sleeve and had Dawn wrap it as a bandage around the wound. He had her tie it tightly to slow the bleeding.

"I've robbed a dozen banks and never been hit by a bullet," he said miserably. "Second time I've been jinxed by a hick town."

Dawn smiled wanly. "Maybe it's telling you it's time to quit."

Walt gave her a funny look.

When the pain began to subside he took several deep breaths and started to relax from the effects of the liquor.

He said: "Dawn, don't know if you noticed, but as we was ridin' over the ridge I spotted a light maybe a coupla miles west. I was thinkin' it might be comin' from a house."

Dawn knew what he was suggesting.

"But are you up to riding?" she asked.

Walt smiled his crooked smile. "Ain't got much choice. Gotta get this thing tended to."

Dawn helped Walt get up on his mount and she did the same. Walt led the way. Although he didn't like the idea of backtracking, even a short ways, he had to get that bullet out before he ran the risk of infection.

As they rode under the trail of moonlight, Walt tried to get his mind off of his pain with conversation.

"Why'd you go agin what I said, Dawn?" he asked, avoiding an accusatory tone.

Dawn had to be firm in her answer. "I—had a feeling . . . a worry that something was going to happen to you. That you weren't going to come out of that town alive. I don't know why I felt that, but I couldn't let you go in there alone."

Dawn's explanation left Walt bewildered. He could not understand such things . . . though he remembered vividly how Dawn had had the same intuition that night her husband Jed had brought the marshal to the farm.

"Reckon you did save my skin. But Dawn, you killed a man back there," Walt said gravely.

Dawn was silent for many moments. She had almost become numb to the memory but Walt's words were a harsh reminder of what she had done. When she opened her mouth to speak, no words came out.

Walt shook his head sadly. "That ain't what I wanted, Dawn. Worse, you not only shot that bank manager . . . you did it in front of witnesses. Ain't gonna be hard for them to identify either of us."

"Wh-what are we going to do, Walt?" Dawn finally found the voice to say.

"Get this bullet pulled outta my arm and just go on with what we planned. We got the money, though it ain't much." He sighed fatalistically. "Well, they been after you as much as me since you sprung me from jail. They already got me pegged as a killer. Don't rightly know if any more killin's are gonna make 'em step up the hunt. No . . . that I don't know."

After they rode on a little farther, Walt turned to

Dawn and said: "Don't know how friendly these folks are gonna be, or how willin' they'll be to help us. Might have to persuade 'em. If so, you'll have to be the one to keep a watch on 'em. Just don't go usin' that gun agin . . .'less you absolutely have to."

Dawn spoke quietly, with what sounded like a tear in her voice. "I won't. I don't ever want to again."

Walt felt intensely sorry for her. He knew she hadn't meant to kill the bank manager. But whether she did or not, it would make no difference to the law. She was as marked as he was now. And if the posse should catch up with them, she'd share the same penalty. Maybe she'd made a fool's move going into the bank. Then again . . . maybe if she hadn't he'd be dead or back in jail. Either way, this time he could not protect her. Once the witnesses were questioned they'd say that it was the woman who had shot the bank manager. Nothing he could say would dispute their claim.

All they could do was keep moving.

What they came upon was a little ranch house, isolated out in the open desert. A lantern was lighted in the front window. There was a small barn out back and as they rode toward it, they could hear the anxious sounds of horses inside, reacting to their approach.

Walt's arm was hurting bad and blood was seeping through the makeshift bandage. He had a high tolerance for pain, but what concerned him was that he was starting to feel weak and a little light-headed, as if he were about to pass out.

As he saw it, the good news was that it was a small-caliber bullet. The bad news was that with the amount of blood he seemed to be losing the slug may have sliced into a vein—or worse, an artery.

Dawn was concerned. She noticed that Walt did not look good. She got him down off of his horse and helped him toward the front of the house.

As they rounded the corner they were greeted by an old man standing on the porch brandishing a scattergun, which was aimed in their direction.

Before the man could say anything, Dawn spoke first, with urgency in her voice.

"You've got to help us, mister. My man's hurt."

The old-timer told the pair to step a little closer, into the light of the lantern that he'd carried out with him, which was seated on the porch. Dawn pulled Walt forward slowly until the man told them to stop. He observed them carefully, his wrinkled face shifting into a variety of suspicious, quizzical, and concerned expressions.

"Please, mister . . . ," Dawn said.

"Been shot, has he?" the man asked gruffly.

There was no point denying what was clearly visible. Dawn replied with a nod.

Walt started to slump against her and Dawn struggled with both arms to keep him upright.

"We're not looking for trouble. Just some help." Dawn quickly added: "We can pay you."

"Ain't interested in money," the man said. "And don't want no trouble, either." Finally he jerked his head toward the open door. "All right, missy. Reckon you'd better bring him inside."

Dawn assisted Walt up onto the porch and into the house. Walt was close to collapsing and the old man put his shotgun aside and lent a hand taking him to a beaten-up sofa, where they laid him down.

Walt's face was pale and he was barely conscious.

"Don't look good," the old man observed.

"Can you fetch me some water?" Dawn asked. "And if you have a sharp knife . . . and something I can use for a bandage."

"Reckon," the old man said. "Though I don't know if it'll do much good."

Dawn didn't want to hear that, even though she herself could see the apparent seriousness of Walt's condition. The wound itself looked minor, just a small hole, but Walt had clearly lost a lot of blood.

She removed the blood-soaked bandage from his arm, and once the old man brought over a basin of water she began to clean in and around the wound. The man then handed her a pocket-knife and watched intently as she dipped the blade into the water then maneuvered it into the bullet hole trying to locate the shell. Though Dawn's brow was perspiring she found herself amazingly calm and not squeamish at the procedure. She knew that this was what she had to do to save Walt and was determined to hold herself together to make sure it was done right.

Finally she felt where the bullet was lodged and carefully pried it out with the pointed tip of the knife. The old man had brought her a jug of whiskey and she poured some into the wound to disinfect it. Finally she wrapped Walt's arm in a clean rag. By the time she was done she looked even paler than Walt.

"You done real fine, missy," the old man said, impressed. "Might be all right after all."

Dawn gave a faint nod. "As long as the bleeding stops," she commented, her mouth gone dry.

"Well, you can stay out here and keep a watch on him," the old man offered. "Try and get some rest and we can talk in the morning. You look plumb tuckered out."

Dawn smiled her thanks and the man disappeared with his whiskey into another room.

She stayed next to Walt and watched as shadow images danced upon the wall, cast by the flickering flame of the table lantern.

Alone and with Walt asleep, Dawn finally felt free to release her emotions. Silent tears flowed as she gave full thought to the man she'd killed today. She could scarcely comprehend that she had become a murderer. She had never intended to shoot anyone, had pulled the trigger only to defend Walt. But no matter the reason or the fact that her action was performed impulsively, without consideration, she now had blood on her hands and it troubled her to think that she may have made some woman a widow, and a child or possibly children fatherless.

Regardless of what happened now . . . whether she and Walt did make it to Mexico and freedom . . . she knew that the memory—and her guilt—would stay with her forever.

She dozed for quick moments, and then she would snap awake. Check on Walt. His breathing was strong and steady, though occasionally his face would contort and he would emit a loud moan, as if he were in the grip of a feverish nightmare. She kept a cold cloth against his head and would frequently remoisten it in the clean water of the basin to also wipe the beads of sweat from his face.

Toward dawn Walt slowly began to waken. Dawn was right there, kneeling beside him, holding his hand. He opened his eyes and looked strangely at her, as though he didn't recognize who she was.

Then, quietly: "Dawn?"

Dawn nodded briskly, barely able to contain her joy at seeing him awake—and knowing her.

"You're all right, Walt," she told him. "The

bleeding stopped . . . and now all you've got to do is get strong again."

"We made it to the house?" Walt asked weakly.

"Yes," Dawn replied, smiling and petting his hand. "You'll have to rest up here for a few days."

Walt's face went troubled. "No. . . . What I mean, Dawn, is you can't stay here. It's—it's only gonna be a matter of time 'fore the posse from Colfax . . . or whoever they send on from Eagle Breach comes this way lookin' for us. They can't find you." He was breathing heavily; what he'd said had taken a great deal of his energy.

Dawn tried to have him not say any more, especially what he was suggesting. But Walt was determined.

He struggled to lift his head and looked squarely at her. "You gotta run, Dawn. I ain't no good now. You . . . you gotta be thinkin' 'bout yourself."

"I'm not leaving you, Walt," Dawn said resolutely.

The shuffled footsteps of the old man crept up behind her.

"Got yourselves in some trouble, I take it?" he said in a neutral tone.

Dawn turned her head slowly to look at him. She didn't answer.

"I figgered as much," the old man said with a sigh.

Dawn said to him: "You've been good to us, mister. We can't ask any more of you."

226

"The law after you?" he asked.

Dawn swallowed and nodded.

The old man heaved a breath. "That puts me in a bad position, don't it? You ride out 'fore your friend's ready and you won't make it too far. You stay here and the law shows up, well . . . that's trouble for all of us."

"He can't be moved," Dawn said. "We just need a day or two for him to get his strength back. I told you, we'll pay you."

The old man snorted. "Missy, money ain't gonna do me much good sittin' in a jail cell."

Dawn's brain worked quickly. "But you don't know us. Who we are. We'd swear to that if we had to."

The old man considered. He looked at Walt and then at the girl.

"That's true enough," he said, scratching the sparse hair on his scalp. "Don't know *who* you two are. Could say you just rode up and needed help. No one could accuse me of any wrongdoin' for wantin' to help a coupla strangers."

"That's all I'm asking," Dawn said, her eyes pleading.

"Well, lemme just ask. Where you ridin' from?"

"Don't tell him, Dawn," Walt urged.

Dawn ignored him. The old man was entitled to the truth. He was their only protection now. She rose to her feet and looked at him straightly.

"Eagle Breach," she responded. "We held up the bank there."

The old man's face never changed expression. "That a fact?" he simply said.

"But—a man was killed," Dawn added softly.

"By him?" the old man asked, jerking his thumb at Walt.

"By me," Dawn said.

"Well, ain't that somethin'," the old man said with a wondering shake of his head. "Met Billy Bonney in New Mexico once. Never knowed no other killer—'specially a woman."

"I didn't mean for it to happen," Dawn explained sincerely.

The old man regarded Dawn sympathetically. "Lookin' at you I can almost believe it, missy. 'Course that won't change things if the law catches up to you. You know that, don't you? Even if you killed him in self-defense, won't hold no ground if you was committin' a crime."

Dawn lowered her face. "I know."

Walt spoke to the old-timer. "Look, now that you know, you gotta talk her into gettin' outta here. They catch her . . . they're gonna hang her."

"Probably so," the man agreed. "Rough country. Swift justice. You two might have a bit of luck on your side, though. Sheriff from Eagle Breach ain't been in town for the week. Rode by here a day or so ago to check up. Said he won't be back 'til this come Sunday."

Dawn looked suddenly hopeful.

The old man added: "That gives you a few days to get back on your feet."

"What about others from the town?" Dawn inquired.

"Naw, they wouldn't be ridin' out nowheres 'til the sheriff gets back. I know them people. Be too scared to go off alone after someone who's done a killin'. Y'see, that kind of thing just don't happen in Eagle Breach."

Dawn looked down with a smile at Walt. "You see—there's no rush. We can stay here until you're better."

Walt's lips pulled down in a frown. "You're forgettin' . . .'bout our other concern," he reminded Dawn.

"Sounds to me like the two of you just got yourselves in a mess of trouble," the old man remarked.

"There's a posse from Colfax chasing us," Dawn acknowledged.

"Headin' this way?"

"Would place a bet on it," Walt said.

The old man looked thoughtful. "City posse's a whole lot different from any that would ride outta Eagle Breach."

"Does that change things—with you?" Dawn asked.

The old man squinted his eyes at her.

"No . . . figger my story would still hold, if you two backed it up."

"That ain't the point," Walt spewed. "Dawn can't be here when they show up."

"We don't know that they will," Dawn argued.

"It's a sure bet they'll stop in Eagle Breach. Once they hear what happened, they'll know it was us. They'll be checkin' out every inch of land. How long d'you think it'll take 'em to find this place . . . standin' out in the middle of the desert like a horseshoe on a coffin." Once again Walt had spoken too much and expended his limited energy.

The old man gazed over at Dawn. "Likely they will show up here, missy."

"Still might not be for a day—or even two," she said with desperate hope.

"I ain't gonna get too far too fast in just a coupla days," Walt told her with bluntness.

"That's a fact," the old man concurred.

Walt spoke gently. "Dawn, here's what I want you to do. Ride outta here. Ride and keep headin' south. Once I can, I'll come after you. Don't worry, I'll find you."

But Walt knew even that was doubtful. He didn't want to alarm Dawn, say anything that might further her resolve to stay, but he suspected that the bullet had done serious damage to his arm. It felt numb. He could barely manipulate the fingers of his hand. The hand he favored when riding a horse.

"I'm not leaving without you, Walt," Dawn stated adamantly.

"Damn it, girl!" Walt erupted.

"Listen," the old man snapped. "All this jawin' ain't gettin' us nowhere. Dawn—that your name? Well, Dawn, you come with me into the kitchen for some coffee. Your friend needs rest, else he ain't never gonna be leavin' here."

Dawn complied. But before she followed the old man out of the room Walt reached over with his good arm and took her hand.

He eyed her with a stern expression. "Dawn, I ain't sure about the old man. You already told him more'n you should. Just don't be givin' him my name."

Dawn looked at him, unsure of the reason for his concern.

"There's a bounty out on me," he explained. "Might give him ideas."

"He told us he isn't interested in money," Dawn returned.

"Mebbe so," Walt said. "But I'll bet he ain't ever seen no two thousand dollars, either."

Dawn smiled in a way that told him she understood. Then she bent over and kissed Walt tenderly on the lips.

"I love you," she said, then lowered her face so that he wouldn't notice her eyes, luminous with forming tears.

Walt wore his crooked smile and with his

good hand placed a finger under her chin and tilted it up so that their eyes met. He rocked his head and winked at her.

The posse from Colfax, guided by the tracking skills of Will Philpott, had checked out the Grady Hills and quickly found traces of Walt and Dawn's campsite. By late afternoon the day following the bank robbery they rode into Eagle Breach. They identified themselves and were instantly informed of the holdup and the killing of the bank manager. A murder they said that was committed by a buckskin-wearing female.

"Egan and the Harley girl," one of the posse remarked. "We coulda prevented this if we hadn't wasted so much time in them hills."

"No one's to blame," Judge Reynolds said. His heart was heavy. He found it difficult to accept that the girl he had allowed into his house and defended was actually the ruthless killer the people of Colfax had accused her of being. But now there appeared to be no doubt.

The posse also learned that the man with her had been shot and wounded and that they rode from town, guns blazing, in a southerly direction. Wasting no time, the posse once more took off in pursuit.

The old man's name was Lem Calloway. He and Dawn had talked for a long while in the kitchen, she with a cup of coffee and Lem pouring straight whiskey into a glass from his jug. He seemed to drink a lot, but Dawn never noticed him acting any differently; there was no change in his speech or behavior. While Dawn had never had much dealings with drinkers, she grudgingly admired his capacity for holding his liquor.

Often during their talk he would scrunch up his expression in deep thought, which added more lines to a face deeply embedded with wrinkles caused by age and probably years out in the sun.

Dawn kept her word to Walt and told Lem that his name was John Cross, even though Dawn felt distinctly that Walt's real identity would mean nothing to Lem. He was a real hermit, a man who claimed to have lived his early years filled with adventure, then who one day decided to go off and live by himself and mind his own business. He had no interest anymore in what went on in the world around him.

Yet Dawn got the impression that Lem had taken a liking to her. She felt that she could trust him—and that included Walt, as well.

But as Lem got serious he did point out to her the wisdom in what Walt was saying. It wasn't smart for her not to move on. And soon. If a posse had trailed them this far, they'd be sure to be checking behind every sagebrush and saguaro cactus, and Lem's farmhouse was not easy to miss.

"I can't be leaving him," Dawn explained with emotion. "Maybe it's something you can't understand . . . but I made myself a promise that I'd be by him no matter what."

Lem tried to look compassionate. He hadn't become so distrustful of people that he couldn't recognize a true love when he saw it.

"You gotta do what you think's best," he offered. "'Course for your own sake I wish you'd reconsider. But it ain't my place to be tellin' you what to do." He started to reach for his glass of whiskey, then pulled his hand back. He chuckled. "I'll tell you, though. If'n you were my daughter, I'd be turnin' you over my knee right 'bout now."

Dawn smiled warmly at him. She stretched out her arm across the table and laid her hand over Lem's dry, bony fingers.

"Wish I *could* have known you before all this ever started," Dawn said almost longingly.

The old man gave a slow nod and tried not to look embarrassed at her affection.

Walt was not one for lying around and once he was awake after sleeping fairly fitfully for however long and feeling somewhat stronger, he got himself up from the battered old sofa to exercise his legs. He was a bit unsteady on his feet at first and still not feeling all together in the head, like the way he remembered he'd felt as a kid recovering from a long stay in bed following a fever. But it felt good to be ambulatory and he

234

was sure he even had some feeling back in his arm. He could just slightly flex his fingers. He wondered, though, if they would ever regain their full dexterity.

He had to get himself back on his feet for another reason. Whether he was up to it or not, he had to get onto his horse. Since Dawn stubbornly refused to leave without him, the only way he could save her neck was to ride off with her.

He walked into the kitchen where old Lem was seated by himself at the table. He told Walt that Dawn had gone outside for a walk to get some air. Walt started to follow when Lem called after him.

"Take a chair and set yourself for a minute," he said, his voice suggesting more of an order than an invitation.

Walt hesitated. There was really nothing he wanted to say to the old man. He was grateful for the help he'd extended but wasn't in the mood for any conversation with him.

"Come have a drink with me," Lem offered.

The jug of whiskey standing on the table looked mighty tempting and Walt sat himself across from the old man. Lem poured Walt a generous cupful of whiskey then refilled his own glass. He raised his drink and Walt did likewise.

Lem took a swallow, released a throaty, satisfied "Ahhhhh" at the taste, then relaxed back in his chair.

"Been drinkin' this stuff for years," he said, licking his lips. "Guaranteed to fix anythin' that's wrong with you."

Walt lifted the cup to his mouth and consumed some of the whiskey. It tasted like native fire-water and he quickly grimaced. He'd drank all kinds of liquor and could handle most, but this stuff was purely potent. He decided to take it easy. His head was still groggy and if he drank any more he wouldn't be good for anything. Yet he marveled at the old man who kept slugging it back like it was water.

"Got quite a kick to it, don't it?" Lem said with a chuckle.

Walt put his cup down on the table. "Think I'll pass. You don't happen to have any smokin' tobacco, I imagine?"

Lem shook his head. "Sorry, son. Never took up the habit."

Walt sat, watching the old man drink his whiskey and saying nothing, but occasionally observing Walt with more than just idle interest.

Walt quickly grew impatient and started to get up from the table.

Lem patted the air with the palm of his hand to get him back into his chair. "No need to rush off. Just wanta have a word with you."

Walt blew out an irritated breath and lowered himself into his seat.

Lem said: "Seein' that you're up and about, I take it you plan to be ridin' off."

"You figger right."

"Maybe none of my business, but what're you gonna do 'bout the girl?"

Walt gave him a tight, narrow stare.

"She's in a heap of trouble," Lem said. "Much as I like her, she can't stay round here, and neither can you. 'Course you'll decide what you've gotta do. But you've gotta make up your mind what's best for Dawn."

"I told you," Walt replied. "We're ridin' out. Today."

"And then what?" Lem asked with a piercing stare.

"We're headin' south. Just like we planned."

Lem sighed. "Your girl Dawn's gonna have a rough road. You both will . . . but I reckon you're used to it."

"I'm used to it," Walt acknowledged flatly.

Lem lifted a withered hand and brandished a finger at Walt. "That girl loves you. So much she's willin' to risk her neck to be with you. I ain't never knowed a love like that. Hell, I ain't never knowed no kind of love at all. But no matter what she and you've done, you gotta stick by her and keep her safe."

Walt couldn't comprehend the point of this conversation, and it rather irritated him. The old man seemed to be lecturing him. But he wasn't telling him anything he didn't already know.

"Listen," Lem said, edging forward across the table. "Got a coupla good horses in the barn. Strong and well fed. I want you and Dawn to take 'em."

Walt gave Lem a quizzical look, then declined his offer with a shake of his head.

"When the posse rides up they'll find our horses and know that we've been here," he explained.

"Ain't got no need for horses anymore," Lem said. "Up 'til recently had a fella come out to keep 'em groomed and exercised. But he's gone and the animals just sit out in the barn. Be a shame to have them fine animals just waste away."

"I told you, we can't be leavin' our horses behind," Walt repeated.

Lem shrugged. "You two ride 'em out aways and shoot 'em."

Walt looked at him blankly, though his words were heavy with disgust at the old man's suggestion.

"I'd sooner put a bullet into a man 'fore I'd shoot a horse," Walt said.

Lem waved his hands in a dismissive gesture. "Then take 'em out into the hills and set 'em free, makes no difference."

Walt mulled this idea over with less resistence. If the posse should come across the two horses running free in the hills it could, at least temporarily, set them off their trail. He changed his mind and accepted Lem's offer.

Walt again started to rise from the table.

"One more thing," Lem said, halting him. "You two are gonna need spendin' money. I've got some stashed away that ain't doin' me much good. Saved quite a lot over the years but just never saw a need to spend it. Would like for you two to take it."

"We got money," Walt told him. "Don't need it."

Lem snapped at him. "I ain't doin' it for *you*, dammit! I want you to have it for the girl—Dawn."

Walt blinked. He regarded Lem with a fixed expression that reflected his doubt. He couldn't figure out the old man's generosity and was frankly suspicious of his motives. Kindness wasn't something he was either familiar or comfortable with, having lived his life being forced into taking what he wanted.

Lem read into his uncertainty. He chuckled to himself. Nothing much had changed since he'd decided to remove himself from society. People were either always too proud or too mistrustful to accept a good deed in the spirit intended.

"I'm an old man," Lem said by way of explanation. "You and Dawn are young and even with all the trouble you got followin' you, you deserve a chance. A chance maybe to get yourselves back on the right path. Dawn in particular. I ain't got that much time left, and if I can help give her that chance, I'd feel that maybe I did somethin' worthwhile with a life not always lived to best advantage. What I'm sayin' is . . . helpin' her would be my privilege."

In an odd sort of way, the old man's attitude made sense to Walt. And he felt a little guilty for having doubted him. In fact, as he saw it now, if he didn't accept the old man's offer, he'd be insulting him.

Walt's expression softened. "Reckon I'd like to shake your hand," he said.

Lem's old, wrinkled face beamed. He accepted the handshake and surprised Walt with the strength of his grip.

"Awright," Lem said, pleased. "Go out and git your girl. Take a look at those horses in the barn and tell me if they ain't the two best ridin' animals you ever saw. While you're doin' that I'll go fetch the money." He paused, added: "Glad we had this time to talk."

Strange old man, Walt thought. But he was sincere in wanting to help them. Walt considered it odd how at this time he and Dawn would meet someone like him. A recluse, yet a man possessed of a genuine goodwill. Was it luck or destiny? Walt hoped it was the latter. Because if that was the case he could believe that he and Dawn had a real chance at making it. Suddenly he was feeling optimistic about their future.

Walt stepped outdoors into a glorious, sun-swept afternoon. Pure white puffs of cloud drifted slowly across the high blue skies. A silky caress carried in the slight desert breeze, and as Walt walked out in the yard toward Dawn he felt rejuvenated.

Dawn turned to him. She was surprised and happy to see Walt on his feet and coming toward her with brisk strides. She noticed how he still held his injured arm stiffly, but other than that he looked fit and healthy. The ruddy color had returned to his face.

She walked over to meet him halfway. She wrapped her arms around his shoulders and kissed him full on the mouth. He encircled her waist with his good arm and pulled her close to him as their parted lips met.

They kissed for a full minute, unaware that old Lem was watching them from the kitchen window, clucking softly to himself.

When they finally ended their kiss, though remaining close in each other's embrace, Walt said: "The old man wants us to take his horses."

"Why does he want to do that?"

Walt smiled. "We'd better saddle up."

Dawn looked a little doubtful. "I don't think you should be riding yet."

"I'm fine," Walt assured her. "Arm's still a bit sore, but I can ride." He spoke honestly. "'Sides,

241

Dawn, you ain't leavin' me much choice."

He debated telling her about the money the old man offered them. Unless Lem himself mentioned it, Walt decided not to say anything until much later. Dawn would surely protest his generosity and that would stall them. And Walt wanted to get moving right away.

The two separated from each other and Dawn started toward the barn. Walt stood where he was for a moment watching her walk, her hips swaying in a naturally enticing way. The look on his face was one of pure admiration. His heart beat with a contented rhythm as he thought about how much he loved her.

Before he could turn to go back inside the house he saw Dawn halt her stride abruptly. She seemed to be gazing at something, off into the distance. Curious, he started to walk toward her when she spun around to face him. Her doe-like eyes were wide, her mouth was open, and her face looked drained of color. She didn't speak, just turned her head back in the same direction as before. Walt's eyes followed.

It was too far to see precisely what had captured Dawn's focus.

But it appeared that men on horseback were coming toward the house.

Chapter Fourteen

"Posse," Walt said, his voice flat, his expression vacant.

Dawn noted the tone in his voice. It disturbed her. It sounded like a tone of resignation. As if he recognized that all hope was gone and he was prepared to give himself up.

"Walt, we have to get outta here," she urged. "There's still time."

Walt looked at her. Without speaking the words his face seemed to express that there might have been time—earlier. But that now they had little chance of outrunning the posse.

"Dawn," he said, taking her firmly by the arm and locking his eyes into hers, "we only got one hope. We gotta fight 'em here. And that's what I'm prepared to do 'cause they ain't never takin' me back to no rope. I don't want that for you neither. Y'gotta know our prospects is slim . . . and you gotta decide for yourself. But that's what I aim to do."

Dawn suddenly looked frightened. The impact of what he was saying hit with full force. He was going to shoot it out with them. He was acknowledging that he would most likely be killed. Now with that possibility so close at hand, the thought of losing him overwhelmed her.

And so she decided that if this was how it had to be, she would die beside him.

Tightly, she clutched him in a quick embrace that she wished would last forever, before Walt tore himself loose to take up position beside the barn. He brushed the sweat from his brow with a swift sweep of his back hand. He only regretted that his arm was useless to put into action the Winchester resting in the scabbard of his horse. He could have used the long-range shots from the rifle to slow the riders before they got too near to the ranch. He just had his six-shooter to depend on.

But he was determined that while they might kill him, he would bring down some of their number.

Dawn dashed inside the house to take the Navy Colt from her handbag. She was met in the front area by Lem, who looked at her sadly.

"They've come?" was all he said.

Dawn gazed at him with sorrowful eyes. "If we can . . . we'll tell them you knew nothing about who we were."

Lem just dropped his head and gave it a shake.

Dawn rushed back outside and saw Walt crouched by the barn, watching the rapid progress of the riders. As she went to be beside him, Walt turned toward her and shouted for her to bring the box of .44 cartridges that he'd placed in the saddlebag on her horse.

Shells in hand, she came back over to him,

keeping low as she ran. She could see the posse clearly now, riding briskly through the clouds of dust whipped up by their horses. The men looked to number more than she would have thought, allowing her little doubt about their determination in bringing them in.

She handed Walt the box of cartridges but he shook his head and instead took the Navy Colt from her grip.

"You let me handle the shooting," he told her. "You just stand ready to reload." He glanced at the Navy Colt, shook his head, and muttered facetiously: "Yeah, Jed couldn'ta picked a better weapon."

In those minutes as the posse continued to advance Dawn almost wished that Walt would simply surrender. At least he'd be alive . . . and though it seemed impossible to her, as long as he lived there was always hope.

"We got the advantage that they don't know we're here. Just need for 'em to get a little closer," Walt said as he lifted his revolver in his good hand and took steady aim.

The hoofbeats sounded louder, almost keeping rhythm with the pulse throbbing at the side of Dawn's head.

And then Walt leaped to his feet, swinging around the side edge of the barn and making himself visible to the eyes of the posse. The sudden-ness of his appearance surprised the men, catching them off their guard, as Walt had intended. Before they could reach for their sidearms Walt fired off all six shots from his revolver, hitting several of the men with his quick yet careful aim; the sudden eruption of gunfire caused many of the horses to rear in fright. While some of the posse held back only momentarily before continuing forward on horseback, now discharging their own weapons, others leaped from their mounts and scrambled toward the barn, likewise covering themselves with their gunfire. Walt handed the revolver to Dawn for reloading while he stepped back to the side of the barn and fired from the Navy Colt. Once the ammo was exhausted he tossed the gun aside. It was of no more use to him. Dawn's hands were trembling, though she worked as fast as she could sliding shells into the Colt. Bullets zinged all around them, a few shots tearing off chunks of wood from the side of the barn where she and Walt were crouched. The men were like an advancing army, closing in on a vastly outnumbered outpost.

"We've got to get inside the barn," Dawn suggested breathlessly.

"Head in there and we'll be trapped." Walt paused. "Hell, we're trapped anyway. Might as well get us some cover."

Dawn had the Colt reloaded and handed it to Walt. As they rose from their crouches Walt fired off two shots that went nowhere but briefly halted the men on foot, and they raced into the barn.

The riders made it into the yard first. Walt and Dawn hid themselves toward the back, huddled together among deep piles of hay. Sunlight filtered in through the cracks in the wall of the barn, reflecting a deep golden glow off the straw. They listened carefully and could hear the hurried rustle of footfalls as the men swiftly dismounted and took up positions on either side of the entrance to the barn.

Then all was quiet for several moments until Judge Reynolds stepped forward and called to them.

"Walt Egan! This is Judge Reynolds from Colfax City. There's no way out. Do yourself and the girl a favor. Give up your guns and walk outside."

No response.

Walt turned to Dawn, smirked, and said in a whisper: "A favor, he says. Don't call hangin' by a noose much of a favor."

Dawn squeezed his arm tightly.

Walt considered the two horses inside their individual stalls, stamping their hooves against the hard earth and rattling their halter chains nervously.

"Dawn, honey," he said, "I ain't never gonna make it. And I'm sorry to say, neither are you. Not if we stay in here. But if I can get on one of them horses and make a rush outside . . ."

"They'll shoot you the minute you get outside," Dawn said fearfully.

"Yeh, maybe," Walt said. "But even if that's so, I much prefer dyin' that way. You know that, Dawn. But look, maybe . . . maybe you still got a chance. They might not be so quick to hang a woman."

"If that's what you're set on doing, Walt, I'm going with you," Dawn said steadfastly.

Walt looked at her sharply. "That's foolish talk."

"No," Dawn protested. "What's foolish is you expecting me to stay back and watch you die."

"Egan!" the voice of Judge Reynolds called again. "We're giving you just two minutes for you and the girl to surrender peacefully. Otherwise we're prepared to burn down the barn and smoke you out."

"Well, that settles it," Walt said with a sigh. He looked at the girl tenderly. "Just know, Dawn, that I ain't got no regrets. I'm glad we was together. Wouldn't change a minute of what we had."

He started to rise, his eyes focused on the two horses, making a quick assessment of which would be the faster. Dawn took him solidly by the forearms, surprising him with her strength and causing him to wince with pain as she pulled on his injured arm.

Walt gazed at her with a long, deep look, as if imprinting on his brain the image of her. He helped her as she started to her feet. He drew her close enough to kiss her . . . and with her guard down, he suddenly shoved her hard so that she toppled back into the hay. Before she could pull herself up Walt had already rushed into one of the stalls. He flung himself onto a horse and directed the animal toward the opening of the barn.

He fastened Dawn with his crooked grin before whipping the horse into a gallop.

"Walt! No!" Dawn screamed.

The horse bolted from the barn. Walt held himself crouched low, his good arm flung around the animal's neck, but as soon as horse and rider were out in the open the posse spun around with their rifles and handguns poised and started firing in a fusillade.

Instantly Walt was hit many times in the back, the impact from each bullet causing his body to jerk upward, and long before he could clear the expanse of the yard he swayed drunkenly on the saddle before spinning off his horse onto the ground.

Dawn burst forward from the barn. A couple of the men quickly grabbed her and she struggled frantically against their grip to get free and go to Walt.

Finally the judge ordered them to let her go.

Dawn rushed over to the fallen Walt. He was lying prone in the dirt and sand, inching his body along in a crablike forward motion with fingers clawing into the grit, scooping and releasing small handfuls. His shoulders and back had been ripped to shreds by the relentless gunfire.

Dawn was alternately screaming and crying as she knelt next to him and gingerly turned him over onto his side. Walt's eyes were wide and looked frightened.

"Oh, Walt, no . . . ," Dawn said, her voice soft and trembling.

A look of calm came over Walt's face as his eyes met hers. He raised his hand to touch the soft skin of her cheek, struggling against the pain of his wounds to give her a smile. He nodded slightly, as if to tell her that it was all right . . . and then his body stiffened in her arms before it relaxed for the last time.

Dawn smiled through her haze of tears as she closed his eyes and looked upon the final expression of peace that rested upon his features.

The posse had moved forward and now stood around her, allowing her these final moments with the dead outlaw. Old Lem Calloway was among them. After a while he stepped apart from the others and took the girl gently by the shoulders, lifting her to her feet. When Dawn could finally look away from Walt she turned to Lem and spoke directly to him, as if no one else was present.

"He's dead," she said softly.

Lem gave his head a slow nod.

And Dawn collapsed sobbing in his arms. He held her in his embrace for a long while.

EPILOGUE

The Day Of . . .

The Colfax courthouse trial had lasted for two weeks. For many it seemed unnecessarily prolonged for such an open-and-shut case. Dawn had no defense although many arguments were presented on her behalf. But as Judge Reynolds presided over the precedings he knew the verdict was never in doubt. Nor could be the penalty. The citizens of Colfax City demanded a punishment that would show they held no prejudice as to the gender of a confessed murderer. Judge Reynolds was a servant of the people and since Dawn Harley was ultimately and unanimously found guilty by the jury and there was no legal precedent to grant her leniency, he could not counter their petition.

As Dawn stood solemnly before him in the courthouse that terrible day, Judge Reynolds ordered her death by hanging. In an eerie echo of what had ensued after Walt Egan's sentencing, the entire packed courthouse cheered. People leaped to their feet, shaking hands with friends and strangers alike and clapping each other on the back.

Dawn just stared at the bench blankly, her face betraying not so much as a twinge of emotion.

Judge Reynolds was so sickened by the spectacle that he didn't even call for order. His work was over. He merely stepped down from the bench and retired to his chambers.

From the time of Dawn's arrest to her sentencing three weeks later significant changes had occurred in Colfax City. Most notable was the appointment of a new marshal, Jake Braddock, to fill the vacancy left by Henry Thornton—and possibly Blackie Collins. Braddock had dealt with a lot of rough characters in his years but he felt completely unqualified to deal with a condemned female, though he tried his gruff best to make sure she was comfortable.

Dawn, in any case, didn't have much to say. She sat silently in her jail cell most of the time. Braddock was considerate in that he kept away citizens who frequently came by the office hoping to get a good look at the first female ever to be hanged in a public execution in Colfax City.

Only toward the end did Dawn make a request. She asked to speak with a newspaperman. She decided that she wanted to tell her story—not necessarily for publication, but because she felt she had to. Hunter Tipton of the *Colfax City Chronicle* was approached and he readily agreed to meet with her.

This was to be Tipton's first and only meeting with Montana Dawn. He listened as she told her story, hastily jotting down notes, and as their afternoon together progressed he began to feel a sympathy for her. Like others in the town, at first Tipton had formed an entirely different opinion of the girl, viewing her only as a criminal, a murderer, and while he naturally could not approve of many of her actions, he began to understand her devotion to the outlaw Walt Egan.

Before Tipton left her jail cell Dawn said to him: "If someday you want to print my story, you have my permission."

Tipton shook her hand and didn't reply. At the time he didn't think he ever would publish it. It was his contention that, true or not, no one would *want* to believe her side of the story.

The legend surrounding Montana Dawn's life and exploits had already started circulating throughout the territory—and beyond.

The day of the execution Judge Reynolds came by to see her. Dawn looked especially pretty, having spent the morning fixing her face and hair. She seemed happy to see the judge, which was not a reflection of how Judge Reynolds was feeling.

They talked superficially for a few minutes, about the weather and what a clear, fine day it was. And how soon it would be winter and if snows might come. They both avoided discussing the matter at hand. To the judge it seemed vulgar and inappropriate. Dawn herself appeared uninterested. The conversation they did have was awkward for the judge. He'd come to the jail intending to say more, but quickly found he didn't have the words with which to properly express what he was feeling: sorrow, extreme regret.

It was as their visit was coming to an end that Dawn finally and obliquely broached the subject.

"It's funny," she said reflectively. "Walt was probably the bravest man I ever knew. Yet he was so afraid of being hanged."

"Are you?" the judge asked mildly.

Dawn looked at the judge and shook her head.

She said quietly: "I've had a lot of people close to me who've died, most before it was their time: my father, mother . . . Jed, Walt. The way I look at it, no matter how you die, the result is the same. It happens to all of us. So . . . no, I'm not afraid."

Judge Reynolds shifted uncomfortably. "Dawn, if it's any consolation, I spoke to the hangman before I came here. He promises me that you won't feel any pain. He'll even be using a special rope, made from silk, he says, so that it'll feel smooth against your skin."

Dawn smiled and seemed appreciative, if unconcerned. But she had one more thing to say to him before he left.

"I'd like to ask you a favor, if you can," Dawn said softly.

The judge nodded. "Of course. If I can."

Dawn hesitated, then she said: "I'd like it if . . . I could be buried next to Walt."

The judge understood. "We can do that, Dawn. Guess it seems . . . kind of fitting."

What he didn't tell Dawn was that her burial plot had already been dug, next to her husband Jed. But he would see to it that her request was granted.

As Dawn was escorted from the jailhouse toward the gallows she was greeted with jeers and cruel comments from those assembled outside. She seemed oblivious to the curses and name-calling and walked with her head held high. Her apparent bravery in the face of her execution gradually sent a hush over the crowd.

Hunter Tipton stood next to two well-dressed strangers whom he recognized were not residents of Colfax and overheard them talking. They were newspaper reporters. Curious, Tipton stepped in a little closer to hear more clearly what they were saying.

He immediately wished he hadn't.

"How's this for a heading: *'Montana Dawn: She Killed Her Husband to Ride With Her Outlaw Lover.'* So we embellish it, throw in some extra bank robberies, maybe another killing or two. No one will care. People back East love this stuff about the West."

"Write it like that and I can guarantee you a book deal," the other man said.

Disgusted, Tipton stepped away and turned his eyes back to Dawn.

She mounted the steps of the scaffold, a firm smile on her lips and with her courage intact. The sun felt warm on her face and she politely requested that the hangman let her enjoy it for just a few moments longer before he placed the black hood over her head. He obliged with a nod of his head, stepping back. Dawn closed her doe-like eyes against the bright, comforting rays of the sun and she sighed contentedly.

While she'd never known whether Walt believed in Heaven or an afterlife, she did. And she knew that despite the mistakes he had made, Walt was a good man, and that God was forgiving. That knowledge gave her solace.

And as she took her final look out into the open country beyond the town, any faint doubt that she may have had was instantly erased as she saw him clearly: Walt, seated atop a proud white steed, leaning slightly forward on his saddle with his black-gloved hands resting on the pommel, Stetson pushed up over his brow so that traces of his black curly hair fell upon his forehead, looking as she would always remember him, smiling at her with his crooked, sideways grin.

He would be waiting for her.

Dawn smiled back—a private smile with tears filling her eyes.

Soon she and Walt would be together—forever.

"One short sleepe past, wee wake eternally,
And death shall be no more; death, thou shalt die."
—"Death Be Not Proud," John Donne